The Cat of Doom

A SURREAL APOCALYPTIC FANTASY WITH POETICAL AND MUSICAL INTERLUDES

I0520259

The Cat of Doom

A SURREAL APOCALYPTIC FANTASY WITH POETICAL AND MUSICAL INTERLUDES

Mark P Henderson

First Published in 2020 by Fantastic Books Publishing
Cover design by Gabi

ISBN (ebook): 978-1-912053-30-8
ISBN (paperback): 978-1-912053-29-2

For Phil and Irene.
Have fun with the songs!

Contents

Preliminary fable

Numerology has become the province of New Age pseudo-mystics so it merits scepticism, even mockery. Nevertheless it has a long and distinguished history in Western culture, dating from the time of Pythagoras (sixth century BCE) and boasting such luminaries as Plato, Johannes Kepler, J. S. Bach and Arnold Schönberg among its adherents. According to taste, therefore, the three philosophers in the following fable might be considered luminaries or pseudo-mystics.

'Why are human societies obsessed by the number twelve?' asked the first philosopher. 'Is it because there are twelve months in a year or because there are twelve inches in a foot?'

After a pause, the second philosopher said: 'Six of one and half a dozen of the other, I reckon.'

There was another pause, and then the third philosopher gave his answer.

'Twelve is the product of Three and Four: the Number of Creation and the Number of Destruction. Jesus had twelve disciples: they *created* a new world religion but one among them *destroyed* its founder. The twelve months of the year encompass the time of Creation or Re-creation we call Spring, and the time of Destruction or temporary Death we call Autumn and Winter.'

He allowed a silence to blossom. Then he said: 'Consider the Pyramid.'

The first two philosophers nodded because the third was very wise. He had a long white beard and lived alone at the top of a mountain. How he found enough to eat in so harsh an environment was a mystery, but it is said that the very wise can find food even on a mountaintop. His two companions supposed they should have understood his advice to 'Consider the Pyramid,' but they didn't.

Why *did* the third philosopher ask them to 'Consider the Pyramid?' Would he have explained the ubiquity of *twelve* differently had there been a fourth philosopher? That is, if the total philosopher count had equalled the alleged Number of Destruction, not the Number of Creation?

～

In the beginning–

–there was nothing. In the end there will be nothing. Between those two – what? Moments? Events? (No: moments are segments of time, and events take place within time, and the beginning and the end are the limits of time and are not segments) – between, then, the beginning and the end there was, is, and presumably will be, *something*. Indeed, *everything*.

An old adage tells us we can't create something out of nothing: *ex nihil nihil venit*. Physicists paraphrase this in conservation laws: momentum is conserved, mass-energy is conserved, and so on. Overall, the universe is conservative, which is no excuse for politicians.

But surely that can't be true. If there was nothing and then there was something, there must be a law of non-conservation of non-being. (Is this bad news for Buddhists?) And if in the end there will be nothing – no mass-energy, no momentum – what price our conservation laws?

The Big Bang and the heat death of the universe are ideas as familiar now to the passenger on the Clapham Omnibus as to the cosmologist, both of whom might deem the foregoing argument spurious. Nevertheless, if *ex nihil nihil venit*, where *did* it all come from?

As the third philosopher in the fable might have observed, creation is rooted in destruction. The painter defaces a white canvas. The architect disfigures a green space. The writer confronts a blank page, and out of nowhere emerges a poem, a story, a doodle, a shopping list, a letter to someone half-forgotten. Blankness is suborned. All is changed, all is in flux. There was nothing and now there's something. And in the future, near or remote, change will cease and there will again be nothing; until the next time.

Creation is change; change leads to destruction; destruction bears the seeds of creation. Only outside the endless cycle of creation and destruction does change cease and everlasting stasis lie.

Which should reassure the doubting Buddhist.

Veni, creator spiritus.

~

A PRE-SOCRATIC DIALOGUE

Time changes this to that,
Mutande non quiescat.
Full fathom five thy father lies
On Ilkley Moor baht 'at.

The stars that serve to light us
Comprise so much detritus;
They flicker on and then they're gone,
Confirming Heraclitus.

The trees wear out the breeze,
The sands exhaust the seas;
From earth to skies all Nature cries
'Get stuffed, Parmenides'.

When earth away shall pass,
Likewise the heavens *en masse,*
Shall we then see what deity
Has made so faux a pas?

Life changes this to that,
Mutande non quiescat.
Full fathom five thy father lies
On Ilkley Moor baht 'at.

~

Dramatis personae (et res)

Cuthbert Fell: An all-round incompetent who despite an understanding of electronics passes unnoticed by almost everyone.

Abdul: Cuthbert's only friend.

Herr Dr von Tür: A psychotherapist obsessed with his patients' psychosexual imbalances.

Big Vince: A shaven-headed, tattooed and pierced Glaswegian enforcer; formerly Professor Vincent Tacitus McGrotty, a distinguished historian.

Gabriella de Clare: A seeker after her True Self; formerly Gerda Ekberg, an authority on Norse sagas.

Selina Crumpett: An embittered person; formerly a champion marathon runner and MI5 agent.

Smiley Crumpett: A plastic garden gnome, Selina's only friend; formerly Smiley Shufflebottom of the Gnome Guard.

Aniles: Selina's True Self.

Patricia: An Anglican priest; formerly Regnarta, a Pagan and witch who could transform herself into a flying rabbit.

Gardner-Carpenter:	A serial killer, necrophiliac, handbag thief and handyman from a non-existent country, whose real name is unpronounceable.
The Mangy Dogs:	The pack includes MD1, pack leader; MD2, his bitch; MD3, their puppy; Jerry Mire, *alias* Grimpen, a gloomy prophet; Sam and Ella, the chefs; and Sniffer Simon, a tracker.
Winston:	A white poplar tree in Selina's garden.
Esmerelda:	A rowan tree in Selina's garden.
Yggdrasilsdottir:	A giant ash tree in the garden of the hidden cottage where Gardner-Carpenter works as handiman.
Bruce:	A seven-legged spider.
Disgruntled blackbird:	An unwilling immigrant to East Sussex.

Various habitués of *The Jolly Jihadi*, an alcohol-free hostelry in Rotting Bishop, East Sussex.

The Cat of Doom:	A cat.

The complexes of Cuthbert

When the star fell into the park, Cuthbert Fell abandoned his cocoa and rushed out to collect it. It took him only moments to build a pen in his garden, and the star found itself enclosed. This, it thought, is what happens when a star falls to earth. But it wasn't afraid because Cuthbert seemed kind.

Cuthbert used the star to light his cigarette. It was classier than a match or even a gold-plated lighter. It would make him the envy of other smokers, though it would be awkward to carry.

He awoke in his sagging armchair. He'd spilled his cocoa.

'What an absurd dream,' he thought, dabbing his trousers with a stained towel. 'I don't smoke.'

The dream had many levels of absurdity. Cuthbert wasn't capable of building a pen robust enough to remain upright in a moderate breeze, especially if it was intended to corral something as wild as a fallen star. In any case, he had no garden. Also, the park wasn't visible from his rented bedsit.

He decided to tell Herr Dr von Tür about the dream. Herr Dr von Tür would interpret it; he was a leading authority on psychosexual imbalances, which he perceived everywhere and in everyone.

Cuthbert had first consulted Herr Dr von Tür because of his problem with doors. He banged his head on every lintel and was therefore obliged to wear an industrial helmet when he left the bedsit. Whenever he entered a building the helmet slipped over his eyes and he tripped over the doorstep. If there was no doorstep he imagined one and tripped over it anyway. This is why he was called Cuthbert Fell.

Visits to shops, concert halls, theatres and museums were full of danger. Automatic doors declined to open when he approached, or they closed as he was passing through and trapped him by the scarf or the coat tails or the supermarket carrier bag, eliciting merriment from onlookers. Such scenes should have embarrassed Cuthbert. Instead, they frightened him. He was afraid of doors.

'Never go to Zanzibar, Cuthbert,' his friend Abdul advised.

After seven consultations – three plus four – involving hypnotic regression, Herr Dr von Tür unearthed the cause of Cuthbert's portaphobia: the wardrobe in his childhood bedroom, a dark oak wardrobe that had glowered and chuckled and housed monsters. At midnight, when the house slept, it would awaken him. He would peer from beneath the blankets and watch its door creak open to reveal impenetrable blackness, within which lurked hungry yellow eyes and dripping mandibles.

Cuthbert's difficulties with doors continued after his portaphobia had been explained but they no longer frightened him. Instead, they embarrassed him.

~

NOT A SONG ABOUT DOORS

I don't think I could write a song
Upon the theme of 'door';
Dreaming up rhymes would take too much time
(Though I can think of three or three plus one,
And maybe several less few).

If I should ask in bar or street
For rhymes to go with 'door',
The chances are I'll only meet
Folk who think I'm a tedious chap,
Jokers who stick in their paddle,
And those for whom it's a task.

A fitting subject for my song
Could be what's *behind* the door;
Options are many, and among
These are crowds of the impoverished,
Mines replete with a mineral deposit,
Food in a mighty stockpile,
A boudoir housing a naughty girl,
A sty containing a male pig,
Or a ghastly scene of shed blood
Covering the deserted carpet.

Looking for inspiration
For a song about a door,
I went to look in libraries
And over books did ponder

To find traditional wisdom
And ancient tales of long ago
Until my eyes grew uncomfortable,
But I couldn't find the nugget in the middle
Of the subject that I vowed
Would never make me emit zeds in my sleep.

⁓

Abdul's guidance

Cuthbert had met Abdul at college. He'd made other acquaintances, too, but they'd forgotten him within minutes. Abdul didn't forget him; he noticed people, and he was patient and tolerant as well as observant. Anti-Muslim barbs seemed never to offend him, even the ones masquerading as jokes. He was open-minded about beliefs and behaviour and he never tore his hair and beard at Cuthbert's all-round incompetence.

'You don't need to see a shrink, Cuthbert,' he said. 'Just get a grip and sort yourself out, like I did. I used to run with a gang. I was up to all sorts, including violent stuff. Then I got myself together and did this history degree.'

It was true: Abdul had run with a gang when he was a teenager, inflicting violence on innocent bystanders, and then he'd become devoutly religious and entered tertiary education. Cuthbert understood this, but he wondered whether recurrent exposure to racist and Islamophobic insults *had* upset his friend, stoical façade notwithstanding, and he was now offering advice by way of retaliation.

'Doesn't it get up your nose,' he asked, 'when people call you "jihadi" and ask where your bomb is?'

Abdul shrugged.

'If you inhale ignorance and prejudice, they choke you. So no, Cuthbert, it doesn't get up my nose because I don't let it. I don't even try to explain what "jihad" means.'

Cuthbert confessed ignorance of the real meaning of

"jihad". The media had a version, but the media were probably as misled about the topic as the readers whose prejudices they fuelled.

'I don't suppose it *really* means random murders committed by gullible young people who've been brainwashed by sick and insane older people.'

'No,' said Abdul, 'it doesn't.'

He said *his* internal jihad was against gambling because he loved to gamble – casino games, horses, football, poker – and could easily become an addict; and against his other main weakness, fornication, which was displeasing to Allah but the strongest of all weaknesses.

'Internal jihad is something you Christians are supposed to do as well, except you call it, like, fighting your inner demons. Right? Internal jihad is what *all* people need to do, but it's easier to fight your demons if you have, like, a strong faith. Less hard, anyway. *Your* jihad should be against your total incompetence, Cuthbert, your inability to stumble through life without serial disasters.'

Cuthbert wanted to know how a word denoting the struggle for personal goodness or rightness had come to be so misinterpreted by the media and the western public. Abdul explained about "external jihad", the obligation to defend family and faith if they're under mortal threat.

'The crazy warped people and the brainwashed gullibilia you mentioned see mortal threats in everything and everyone who doesn't share their narrow interpretation of Islam. So they launch random attacks in the deluded belief that they're defending something that needs to be, like, defended.' Abdul shrugged again. 'Sickoes of that sort pervert all the best we have in values, attitudes, beliefs, practices, whatever. And perverted ideas will always ensnare people who consider themselves, like, marginalised, downtrodden, alienated, overlooked ...'

'So you don't believe these self-styled jihadists who want to destroy western society are genuine Muslims,' said Cuthbert.

Abdul lit a cigarette with a gold-plated lighter, having no fallen star about his person, and then said yes, they *were* genuine Muslims, although decent Muslims disowned them.

'Look at Christian history, Cuthbert. Spanish Inquisition, right? What the inquisitors did to so-called heretics wasn't Christian in the eyes of most Christians. Right? But the inquisitors *were* Christians. They were just fanatics who espoused a, like, *perversion* of Christianity. Well, these self-styled jihadi gangs – Al-Qaida, Islamic State, Boko Haram, Al-Shabir, the Taliban, and all the rest – they're, like, Islam's Spanish Inquisition. They're jerks and knob-heads, but they're *devout* jerks and knob-heads.'

Cuthbert wasn't satisfied with the analogy. He wondered why more people today wanted to become self-styled jihadi thugs than had ever sought to become inquisitors. However, before he could inquire further, Abdul had gone on to bewilder him with an argument about faith and hope in salvation versus submission to God's will ('The main difference between our two religions when it comes down to it,' said Abdul, 'though Islam and Christianity are a hell of a lot more similar than the fanatics on either side admit'); and how, in the west, faith and hope in God had segued into faith and hope in human scientific and political endeavour while Islam remained the religion of submission and obedience, so now it was all tied up with the incompatibility between democracy and freedom on the one hand and Sharia Law on the other, between human rights and religious tradition.

'So you can't be surprised that a lot of my Muslim brothers and sisters have mediaeval leanings.'

Abdul loved all things mediaeval, especially tales of European chivalry and knightly deeds. He loved the King Arthur romances most of all.

Cuthbert thought about it. 'Well, why should Abdul's religion debar him from enjoying Arthurian tales?' he asked himself. Then it occurred to him that untold numbers of Christians have revelled in *The Thousand Nights and One Night*; what, morally speaking, was the difference? The analogy pleased him. Perhaps the Arthurian tales could be viewed as jihad stories, he thought; both external and internal jihad, because as well as seeking to correct their own failings, the Knights of the Round Table rode forth and used force of arms to combat whatever they perceived as evil in the world. 'Maybe that's why Abdul likes the stories so much,' he decided, 'and is fascinated by mediaeval European history. And he's right about my needing to struggle against constitutional incompetence. The trouble is, whenever I try, I fall over.'

~

THE KNIGHT WITH SMELLY FEET

Hey ho merrily ding dong bell,
A knight loved a maid and he loved her well;
'If you fancy me,' said he, 'then we
Will hey ho merrily wedded be.'
But the maiden turned her face away
And said, 'Come back some other day;
A knight like you is all very well,
But I won't marry you for your feet do smell.'

Away rode the knight, forlorn and sad;
'Twas true, two smelly feet he had,
And they didn't smell like the summer rose –
Even his horse wore corks up its nose.
Said the knight as he rode through meadows sweet,
'I'll have to wash these smelly feet,'
So down he got and took off his bootsies
And into the mill stream dabbled his tootsies.

The mill wheel groaned, the mill pond stank,
The geese fell sick and the ducks all sank,
The scum on the water turned thick and green,
But the knight's two feet were lovely and clean.
'Oh ho,' said the maid, 'come back, my dear,
Now that my nose can bear you near,
For I love you well now your feet don't smell,
Hey ho merrily ding dong bell.'

Cuthbert's dreams are interpreted, but the interpretations afford him scant solace

Notwithstanding his half-resolution and Abdul's guidance, Cuthbert consulted his psychotherapist again. Herr Dr von Tür explained that the dream of the fallen star was a wish-fulfilment, common among life's irredeemable failures. The star represented the challenges Cuthbert's unconscious strove in vain to overcome. The cigarette, for which he had no use, was a sexual symbol. It was all quite elementary.

The psychotherapist knew Cuthbert was never destined to tread the Halls of Success. Many people fail to stand out in a crowd but Cuthbert didn't stand out even when he was alone. He'd have appeared only as a minor character in his autobiography. He merged with the wallpaper. You'd think the room was empty. Abdul was one of the few who ever noticed him.

Cuthbert's only skill lay in electronics. His designs were inventive. When he found someone competent and willing enough to construct them according to his specifications, such as Abdul, they worked. During his college days he'd had difficulty awakening in the morning; alarm clocks had no effect. To overcome the problem he connected his bedside clock via a battery to a bell at the far side of the room, so that when he switched off the alarm this more distant bell would ring and he'd have to climb out of bed and cross the floor to silence it. This would activate a third bell above his bedroom door. By the time he'd switched off the third bell, he conjectured, he'd be awake. He tested the system and it worked.

On the morning after he'd installed this system, his alarm clock rang and he opened a bleary left eye. Realising that if he switched off the alarm he'd be obliged to stagger around the room deactivating the other two bells, he reached up, tore out the wires and went back to sleep.

'Cuthbert,' said Abdul, 'you're a dick. You're destined to be cast into the bottom drawer of life with the rest of the world's detritus. Use your skill. Fight your demons.'

Cuthbert's masterpiece was the self-abnegator. The self-abnegator was a box with a lid, a power supply, an adjustable timer and a switch. You could attach the box to the wall or stand it on your desk or your coffee table. When you switched it on, nothing happened for a while, depending on the timer setting. Then the lid opened and a mechanical arm emerged. The arm flexed. Its fingers found the switch and returned it to the 'off' position. Then the arm retreated into the box and the lid closed. It all happened quite slowly.

There was a potential market for self-abnegators in university philosophy departments and among certain religious groups. They thought it symbolised the cycle of life, planetary evolution, the birth and death of the universe. Existentialists wallowed in its pointlessness. Buddhists valued it as a teaching tool. Someone wanted to install a self-abnegator in her home to serve as a conversation piece. Abdul found it amusing. Others considered it a waste of space-time, like its inventor.

Expectations were never satisfied. Cuthbert left the

prototype of the self-abnegator on a seat in St Pancras Station while he went to the loo. The bomb disposal team destroyed it in a controlled explosion. Cuthbert failed to obtain his degree. He was unemployed.

◆

Before he'd met Herr Dr von Tür, Cuthbert had supposed dreams to comprise fragments of the past reflected in the mind's distorting mirror. This is a common supposition, though New Age types regard dreams as distorted reflections of the future, a belief caused by a mutation in the critical thought gene. Cuthbert wasn't a New Age type and didn't carry the mutation. Youth notwithstanding, he was an Old Age type.

However, he'd once consulted a psychotherapist called Janua about a recurring dream. This dream had taken him to an unfamiliar place, perhaps a seaside resort, with a woman he'd known at school and didn't like. The woman he didn't like was called Patricia, though in her earlier life as a Pagan and a witch she'd used the name Regnarta, which was almost but not quite *étranger* spelt backwards and had a first syllable connoting authority by divine right. Regnarta said she could transform herself into a flying rabbit during certain phases of the moon. Her coven told her that a flying hare would be more traditional but she was of independent mind. Her youth behind her, Patricia, *alias* Regnarta, had changed her religious affiliation and had been ordained as an Anglican priest. Cuthbert had met her twice in waking life during the previous year, presiding at funerals.

In the dream he was holding hands with her. He took her to an outdoor café and bought her a drink but he couldn't sit down: the first chair he tried was taller than an old-fashioned laboratory stool so he towered over both her and the table; the second was a toy from a child's play-house. He couldn't obtain a cup of tea because other patrons had used up the hot water, so he took a mug and a tea bag indoors to solicit the manager's help. In the poky office, which was lined with institutionally-coloured tongue-and-groove wood and lit by a single grimy window, the manager's assistant begged him for a critique of his abstract paintings. The paintings were of dubious quality so Cuthbert was diplomatic. When at length he returned to the outside world with cup of tea in hand his companion had gone.

'The dream symbolises both past and future,' said Janua the psychotherapist. It was Cuthbert's second consultation with her. The first had been unproductive because she hadn't realised he was there. 'Have you been driving a car with a woman's hat on the passenger seat during the past week?'

'How did you know?'

'It's obvious. What you need is a new car.'

'What make and model would you suggest?'

Janua waved the question away with a bejewelled right hand. 'Irrelevant. But the vehicle must be canary yellow.'

Cuthbert couldn't afford a new car. Indeed, he shouldn't have been driving the old one with the woman's hat on the passenger seat. He'd failed his driving test.

◆

After he'd consulted Herr Dr von Tür about the dream of the fallen star he found a letter pinned to the door of his bedsit by a poisoned Amazonian arrow. The letter was from the Merchant & Grendel Enforcement Agency. It read:

Dear Mr Fell,

We are advised that as of the 13th inst. your rent arrears stand at £3650.00. We request that you pay this amount in full, plus our 10% agency fee (total sum due = £4015), to the above address on or before 12.00 noon on the 24th inst.

If you are unable to meet this deadline, Big Vince and a couple of his mates will call upon you to explore alternative courses of action. We use the word 'deadline' advisedly.

Yours sincerely,

G. B. H. Merchant,

Director.

Had Abdul not been in Saudi Arabia for the Hajj, Cuthbert would have sought his advice before fleeing for his life. But Abdul wasn't answering his mobile phone and wasn't expected home until well after twelve noon on the twenty-fourth inst. So Cuthbert packed all his possessions into four supermarket carrier bags and piloted his rusty Volkswagen to pastures new.

He'd painted the car canary yellow using cut-price household gloss from B & Q. The woman's hat was still on the passenger seat.

~

MERCHANT & GRENDEL: ENFORCEMENT AGENTS

Established back in the 1950s,
Merchant & Grendel ignore the thrifty,
But when debts to local authorities are due –
To private or commercial landlords, too –
We provide enforcement nationwide
Take debt recovery in our stride,
Embrace a philosophy of continuous improvements,
Inducing in debtors bowel movements,
Ensuring for our clients professional delivery,
Making their debtors all quaky and quivery,
Supporting corporate fair debt policies,
Acting without redundant courtesies,
Always ethical, always professional –
Our interview room is the debtor's confessional.
For us, it's not just about collection,
It's about dissuasion and correction.
Our methods might date from times of mythology
But now they're refined by modern technology.
We stand for quality, we're consistent:
Debtors we pursue are never persistent.

(See the following links for details of our Quality
Accreditation, Environmental Accreditation, Contractors'
Health and Safety Certification, Information Security
Management, and Environmental and Corporate Social
Responsibility Statements.)

~

The simplicities of Big Vince

Big Vince's middle knuckle rapped on Cuthbert's door, which buckled. The bedsit responded with an empty echo. Big Vince sighed, causing the tattoos on his chest to flex their muscles, and went to ask Cuthbert's erstwhile neighbours where his quarry was hiding. None of them knew because they seldom saw Cuthbert, even when he stood before them. Big Vince asked them to contact Merchant & Grendel if they chanced to notice him. He gave each neighbour a business card bearing the firm's logo: knuckleduster and crossed jackboots.

He went outside and made three phone calls while the sun gleamed on his shaven pate. The tattoos on his arms had even bigger muscles than the ones on his chest and his piercings glistened. He looked around the litter-strewn environs of the bedsits and grinned, exposing an array of metallic teeth interspersed with gaps. The place looked as though it had been hit by a falling star.

His steel-toe-capped boots trundled him back to his Aston Martin, where he sat behind the wheel and waited. Presently his phone rang. He listened to the message and scribbled something on the back of the latest issue of *History Today*. This issue contained an article by Professor Eima Nowall about the social role and status of philosophers in Classical Athens. Big Vince wasn't impressed. He deemed the article a load of crap about a load of long-dead wankers, written by a living wanker.

'Aristophanes wiz right aboot yon shower o' useless

Athenian jerks,' he said, quoting one of his own lectures. '*Nephelokokkygia*. Cockaigne. *Wolkenkuckucksheim*. Cloud Cuckoo Land. He'd ae put Eima Nowall i' the same place. Nae use fir wankers, Aristophanes hadnae.'

He pondered over the words he'd scribbled on the magazine, grinned again, lifted a pewter flask from the glove compartment, drank from it, opened the driver's door, vomited on to the street and gave a contented sigh. The contents of the pewter flask were non-alcoholic because Big Vince had given up drinking, but they exerted a satisfactory emetic effect. Being sick, calling to Ruth through the big white telephone, boaking, puking, throwing up, indulging in liquid laughter: it was Big Vince's greatest pleasure. He'd extolled the delights of vomiting in many songs. He sang them to the accompaniment of his mandolin, causing audiences to dwindle.

$\sim$

THE ECSTASY OF REVERSE PERISTALSIS

When tragedy and woe are rife
Within this world of grief and strife,
We all are tempted now and then
To glean some pleasure out of life.
I think you will agree again
That of enjoyments we obtain,
Of joys wherewith we can be blessed,
The simplest pleasures are the best;
And I maintain, of everything
That greatest happiness can bring,
The thing I most delight in doing
Is bending o'er the bog and spewing.

I do not mean the sort of spew
That seems to rip your chest in two,
The spew that's dry and grim with pain,
The retching that is retched in vain;
I've never pleasurably spewed
When long deprived of drink and food.
But after some night's heavy boozing,
Bladder full and bowels oozing,
Full of song and yet half-dead
With singing ears and spinning head,
Oh, with what joy my spirit burns
When all that I've consumed returns!

It comes back warm and smooth and sour,
An opalescent yellow shower,

And lies, a pool of steaming goo,
With here and there a lump or two,
For food I've eaten long ago
May be forgot, but even so,
Its progress down the bowel arrested
Appears anew and half-digested.
The sight is wondrous to behold,
Congealing, growing slowly cold,
And my stomach is so empty then
I want to drink it all again.

So when you'd fain escape awhile
From humdrum life and long to smile,
When sorrows of the world you feel,
Then go and eat a hearty meal;
And then, to make your dreams come true,
Just drink and drink until you spew.

Gabriella de Clare's quest

Gabriella de Clare met a man with two pseudonyms who'd journeyed to Sniggerswick from a place that didn't exist. It would have been love at first sight had she known what to call him and if he could have invited her to a real-world home. In the event it became something else at first sight, and afterwards she called him by more than two names, and wished him to a destination that shared the ontological status of his fictitious homeland, evincing no desire to accompany him.

Gabriella de Clare of Sniggerswick wasn't the first woman to learn that men with two pseudonyms and no real place of origin can't be trusted, and she won't be the last. What he took from her she could never recover. She had to buy a new handbag.

But she'd learned from the experience: she needed to find her True Self. She'd changed her forename from Gerda to Gabriella and her surname from Ekberg to de Clare but it hadn't worked; her Self remained partly False. Those who understood such matters told her that the only way to ensure success in the search for one's True Self was to travel by bicycle; so, being of Norse descent, she resolved to become a Biking Viking.

She purchased a bicycle, put her new handbag into the basket, ate a Chinese meal, and then drowned her misery about the man with two pseudonyms under a copious admixture of wines and spirits. This made her sick. She didn't enjoy being sick. In that regard, as in her deficiency of tattoos and piercings, she differed from Big Vince of the Merchant & Grendel Enforcement Agency.

◆

Gabriella rode away from Sniggerswick to search the world for her True Self. The bicycle's wheels orbited their hubs like squeaky planets. 'My wheels are slightly elliptical,' she said. 'So are the bike's.'

Everywhere she went she asked whether anyone had seen her True Self. She asked passers-by. She asked in bicycle shops, in cafés where she stopped for tea and nibbles, in hotels and doss-houses where she spent nights.

'No, we haven't seen your True Self,' everyone told her. 'Have you tried asking a psychotherapist?'

So she visited Herr Dr von Tür. He didn't ask her about her dreams, so the consultation gave her neither need nor opportunity to tell him about her recurrent nocturnal vision, which involved a locked leather case containing a mysterious metallic object. She found the dream exciting but unsettling. Instead, he asked why she *wished* to find her True Self.

'Don't you wish to find yours?' she said.

Herr Dr von Tür considered the question. Then he considered the question some more. He did nothing but consider it. After a while he was admitted to an institution for the bewildered and given a meal, which he scrutinised. He feared he was suffering from a psychosexual imbalance.

Gabriella rode on. Her quest seemed endless. Sometimes, in despair, she drank but eschewed vomiting. Then, feeling renewed, she resumed her journey. In restaurants and bars and public houses she asked: 'Have you seen my True Self?'

'No, we haven't seen your True Self,' everyone told her. 'Why don't you take a nice long holiday?'

So she took a nice long holiday. On the beach in Bali she thought she saw the person she sought.

'Excuse me,' she asked, 'are you my True Self?'

'No, Gabriella, I'm not,' said the woman. 'I'm someone else's True Self.'

'May I ask whose?'

'I'm the True Self of Selina Crumpett of Rotting Bishop, East Sussex, England. If you wish to find *your* True Self, why don't you consult the wise philosopher who lives at the top of the mountain?'

So Gabriella cycled to the top of the mountain and asked the wise philosopher where she could find her True Self. The wise philosopher tugged his long white beard and said in order to fulfil her quest she must stop looking outwards towards her Self, True or Otherwise, and instead look inwards towards the Universe so she might perceive its fate, and hers. Pretending to understand, she mounted her bicycle again and rode away, trying to look inwards towards the Universe. It was a long bike ride over valley and mountain, hill and dale, desert and ocean, and throughout the journey Gabriella kept trying to look inwards. But as any wise philosopher could have told her, beard or no beard, you can't look inwards towards the Universe and cycle safely at the same time. Multitasking has its limits. A careless motorist forced her off the road and she collided with a tall white poplar tree called Winston.

Winston stood at the south-western corner of the garden of Forlorn House in Rotting Bishop, Sussex, England. The south-eastern corner of the same garden was occupied by an injured rowan called Esmerelda. Between the two trees stood a garden gnome called Smiley, who watched the bicycle crash and cried to the owner of the house for help. The owner was Selina Crumpett.

Karma had graced the situation with the kind of symmetry that Cuthbert's acquaintance Patricia, formerly Regnarta, would find characteristic of the convoluted ways of God. Selina had injured Esmerelda; Winston, who had witnessed the assault, had injured Gabriella; Gabriella lay unconscious, wrapped in chestnut paling; Selina was obliged to nurse Gabriella back to health and repair the fence; and Gabriella, if and when she recovered, would recognise Selina as the woman whose True Self she'd encountered on a beach in Bali. Then she'd panic about her bicycle and handbag and complain about drivers who cause accidents.

She failed to recognise the social value of drivers who cause accidents, though in the fullness of time she was destined to attain great wisdom, notwithstanding her lack of long white beard.

～

TWO ENVIRONMENTAL CONCERNS

The conservationists preach desperation
As they ponder the increase of world population,
And loud is their misery, torn is their hair,
As they see motor traffic increase everywhere;
But instead of two problems wherewith we are cursed,
Think of the second as solving the first;

For as traffic increases, you'll find overall
The pedestrian's chance of survival is small,
Since crossing the road at a junction or bend
Is likely to win him a red sticky end;
Pedestrian crossings are more of a worry –
A driver might stop there unless in a hurry.

The victim will find that his entrails have spread
Over quite a large area; moreover, he's dead.
His face is of previous appearance bereft
And a tyre-track is now the sole feature that's left.
Such remains are most useful if left well alone:
They make a smooth surface, save for odd bits of bone.

Then as accidents mount, population decrease
Will cause traffic to dwindle, decline, even cease,
For among the deceased will be loads upon loads
Of drivers whose vehicles were once on the roads.
Since in this the answer to both problems lies,
Let's encourage the accident figures to rise.

So if you're inclined to preach conservation
And long for a lowering of world population,
After each road disaster encourage survivors
To create more road transport and more reckless drivers;
Or to set an example both good and complete,
Volunteer as a victim and resurface the street.

A hiding place

There's a cottage beside the coastal path, overlooking the strand, with a garden that glows with alyssum in spring and hydrangeas in summer. The buddleias around its borders are turbulent with butterflies; a sad man counted twenty-three different species there one sunny July morning. At the bottom of the garden rises a giant ash tree, a refuge for green woodpeckers and red squirrels; its roots pierce to the centre of the earth while its topmost branches caress the sky. Between the ash tree and the cottage is a well of unknown depth. A faint sulphurous odour rises from it.

The cottage is a long single-storey dwelling and stands isolated, invisible from everywhere except the garden gate. Ferns grow from its thatch and grey and yellow lichens adorn its sandstone walls. Tiny windows reflect sun and cloud, and the susurrus of waves on the foreshore lulls the lawns into timeless somnolence. Beside the door stands a stone mushroom on which the occupant could sit and absorb the warmth of the sun, the scent of the flowers and the humming of bees – if there were an occupant.

Walkers on the coastal path admire the idyllic cottage and garden as they pass the gate, but they linger only briefly before moving on. Few venture to step on to the path that beckons them to the low oak door beneath the twittering eaves. Even strangers sense that no one has lived there for a long time. Who maintains the fabric, tends the garden and keeps the path clear? No one asks.

Cuthbert piloted his rusty yellow Volkswagen along a twisting lane past a farm owned by a pack of mangy dogs, who spoke in chorus, a talking blues. The twisting lane became a rough track, which Cuthbert approached too quickly, forcing a cyclist off the road and into a white poplar tree. Shortly afterwards his car fell into a ditch and he tumbled out and continued his journey on foot, carrying his worldly goods in four supermarket carrier bags, leaving the woman's hat on the passenger seat. A few minutes later he found the hidden cottage, opened the gate and wandered up the path. The front door key lay on top of the stone mushroom, shining like a fallen star.

He let himself in, banged his industrial helmet on the lintel, tripped over the doorstep and made himself at home. Far behind him, the chanting of the mangy dogs continued.

~

THE MANGY DOG TALKING BLUES

We're mangy dogs in a close-knit pack
And we take and eat whatever we lack
We ain't got charm so if you chance your arm
By causing harm too near our farm
You're gonna get what's coming to you
And you ain't gonna like what's coming to you
'Cos we run this farm and we run it for us
And our boxers and pugs are pugnacious
You take us on and you're gonna lose
As we talk the mangy dog talking blues

We're noisy and smelly and we won't change
'Cos we're mangy dogs that are dogs with mange
We don't much care if our ways estrange
Folk we don't want here who try to arrange
To have us expelled from our Mangy Dog Farm
And forget the words of Omar Khayyam
So we'll work our land and we'll raise our pups
And cheer our pack as we lift our cups
For we've riches enough and bitches enough
To have no need for civilised stuff
And we'll live the life that's the life we choose
And talk the mangy dog talking blues.

~

In the kitchen Cuthbert found an electric kettle, filled it with water at the sink, plugged it in and switched it on. He opened cupboard doors and drawers. He found pots and pans, crockery, cutlery, coffee, tea bags and sugar. He opened the fridge. It contained three supermarket ready-meals, stale bread, butter, a pound of yellow cheese, an almost-empty jar of raspberry jam and half a carton of lumpy milk.

Someone must live here, he thought. Well, provided they don't expect me to pay for food or lodgings I don't suppose they'll mind. From each according to his ability, etcetera. I hope they've no ties with Merchant & Grendel. He made a cup of black coffee, charred two slices of bread in the toaster, threw them into the garden and ate a piece of cheese.

On the bedroom wall hung two photographs: one of a moustachioed Edwardian gentleman with a tweed jacket and a shooting stick, the other of Mount Ararat. There was a chest of drawers with a trio of teddy bears on top; the drawers were empty except for mothballs and a ticket to a performance of *Brigadoon* in Eastbourne four years earlier. There was also a wardrobe, which contained no clothes. The only items in the wardrobe were a spare blanket, a seven-legged spider called Bruce, and an electronic device of a kind Cuthbert had never seen. It was pyramidal. He studied it but couldn't ascertain its purpose, so he plugged it in and switched it on. It made a whirring noise. A red light flashed and there was an odd smell.

Then he turned round and saw the cat. It was a large, black, silent cat. It lay on the chequerboard tiles and its posture betokened both imminent slumber and imminent pounce, antitheses only a cat can reconcile. It stared at him, a *Felis* devoid of *domesticus*, its yellow eyes opening on depths beyond the limits of the cosmos, beyond the limits of time.

From the bottom of the garden beside the coastal path came a rushing of wind among branches. Around the cottage a gentle zephyr breathed, strength two, but the wind at the top of the giant ash tree was strength seven.

The cat went on staring at Cuthbert. Cuthbert dropped his coffee cup. It broke. The cat didn't move.

'Oh dear. My mother always called me "Butterfingers", said Cuthbert.

The cat went on staring. Cuthbert went back through the kitchen to the living room. The cat was lying on top of the television, staring at him. He still hadn't seen it move.

He wished Abdul were with him to pour cold water on his anxiety. And on the cat.

~

BUTTERFINGERS

'Butterfingers,' said my mother;
I looked at them, and so they were:
Eight butterfingers, two butterthumbs,
Glisteningly greasy, covered with crumbs,
Salted on one hand, fresh on the other,
Ten little portions of long yellow butter.

The cat came in hungry, I fed her a thumb,
I sucked at a pinkie 'til it was gone;
Then in the morning, the worst of my fears:
A hot sun. My hands wept buttercup tears.

Butterfingers? Right on.
I am unhanded, undone.

~

The sorrows of Selina

Selina Crumpett was thin and upright so her spine was like a comb. That morning she'd risen to celebrate what would have been her fortieth wedding anniversary had the wedding taken place. The sunrise mocked her. A blackbird sang on Esmerelda, the rowan tree at the end of her garden. She lifted her twelve-bore shotgun and fired both barrels at it.

She recalled the sweet song the blackbird had sung forty springtimes ago as the limousine bore her to church. The recollection filled her mouth with the flavour of rotting crow, *fillet de corbeau pourri*. Her wedding dress had been pure white, square cut at the neck, yards of lace. All had been well; the sun had shone; everyone invited had attended. Except the bridegroom. She'd run from the church and torn off her engagement ring and flung it down on the nearest gravestone and stamped on it, breaking the heel of her white shoe, ripping the ruby from its setting and flattening the gold circlet. Ruby. Ruby unwedding.

She looked out of the window and apologised to Esmerelda, who'd taken the brunt of the shotgun blast. The blackbird had flown away and was now singing from Winston the white poplar. Was it possible for the abused and shattered to take wing again? She put down the shotgun and went to make her morning cup of coffee. She pulled a cashmere sweater over her underwear and threads snagged on her vertebrae like plastic bags on a seaside breakwater.

In her sitting room were display cabinets full of memorabilia: silver cups, medals, shorts and tops with logos and numbers and insignias of affiliation. Collectively they proclaimed skill, attainment, commitment, pride. She gazed at her running shoes. Not the new pair, the ones she'd worn for last year's half-marathon, but the old pair, the ones that in the eye of imagination still reflected the flash of cameras and the gratification of gold. The soles were worn thin where the balls of her feet had sprung over and again from the track, half the grips were gone and the heels were eroded. One lace was missing. The uppers were discoloured, the white and navy blue weathered to yellow-grey and umber, the stitching burst around the sides; and the material of the left shoe's upper had been stretched and thinned below the proximal joint of the great toe by the pressure of the incipient bunion that had degraded gold to silver, and then to bronze, and then to nothing. The new shoes showed no deterioration. She seldom wore them.

From the end of her garden came the sound of a bicycle hitting a tree and a cyclist smashing into the chestnut paling fence that bordered the coastal path. There was a gnomic utterance: '*Selina! Some dumb bum's driven into Winston!*'

Yes, it was possible for the abused and shattered to take wing again. But if one tried one was likely to plummet.

The blackbird sang a disgruntled song about the lack of peace and quiet in Rotting Bishop, and how much more tranquil life had been in Sniggerswick, and wishing he'd never moved from Sniggerswick, but what could a chap do when his wife insisted because her mother needed sea air, and in any case (his wife had added) it would be healthier for the nestlings, and one tree was as good as another as far as marking territory was concerned, and *her* father would never have moaned about a few low-flying twelve-bore pellets, so what gave *him* the right to complain?

It was a long song. Long and disgruntled.

But the trees weren't interested. They'd been Summoned: from the garden of the hidden cottage the branches of the giant ash tree had called to them, strength seven.

'We hear you, Daughter of Yggdrasil,' murmured Winston the white poplar.

'Speak to us, Yggdrasilsdottir,' whispered Esmerelda the Rowan, attentive despite her shotgun injuries.

'Convey Our Message to the Gnome, Guardian of the Gateway of the Chthonic, who stands betwixt you,' commanded the ash tree.

~

Gabriella's dreams: dialogue in a drawer, and the battle between Moses and St Jerome

Gabriella de Clare awoke in another unfamiliar bed in another unfamiliar room. The quest for her True Self had made the experience familiar. She was sure she was alone, yet soft voices spoke nearby:

'It's been a long time.'

'Yes.'

'Is this it?'

'I guess it is. We're the forgotten ones. The detritus of life.'

'Do you suppose we'll ever see the light of day again?'

'We can see enough. It'll be best if we don't see the light of day. Think what it could mean.'

'It would mean someone had opened our drawer. But if someone opened our drawer they'd be looking for something specific. They wouldn't notice us.'

'No one would open this drawer unless they were preparing to clear it out. I mean, what is there in here for which anyone in their senses could be looking? And if they were preparing to clear out the drawer it would be bad news for us.'

'You're too pessimistic. See that old green tobacco tin with the odd assortment of buttons in it? The drawer-opener might be looking for a button. Or a stick-on sole for a size thirteen shoe.'

'You're grasping at straws. Come to think of it, there's a

packet of drinking straws in the far corner, next to that wooden box full of wax crayons and broken chessmen. You think anyone might open the drawer to grasp a drinking straw or a wax crayon or a broken chess piece?'

'All things are possible. Not all people who open drawers are in full possession of their senses. And some people open drawers at random, with no plan in mind.'

'Hoping for a surprise?'

'Yes, possibly. A surprise.'

'You mean, like being overcome with excitement on happening upon a two year old supermarket receipt?'

'People collect all kinds of things. Don't give up hope!'

'Argue the case any way you like, I believe if we ever see the light of day again we're in trouble. I don't care whether it's a crazy person, or a random seeker after surprises or an eccentric collector, no one will wish to keep an unpaired cufflink and a single sock.'

Half-dozing, Gabriella wondered whether she'd dreamed the dialogue in the drawer. She decided she must consult Herr Dr von Tür again when he'd recovered from his indisposition, and she from hers.

Then she fell back into the arms of Morpheus and dreamed a different dream.

◆

Moses and St Jerome were about to come to blows. And they were soaked. Despite the rain, Gabriella took a photograph: the saturated hair and beards, the dripping cloaks, the soggy sandals and the furiously locked eyes and clenched fists amused her more than anything she'd seen since the dog had tried to chase a cat down Sniggerswick High Street and pulled over the metal litter bin to which it had been secured. Being attached to the dog's lead the fallen bin had pursued the unfortunate canine, banging and clanking, monstrous and metallic. The dog's owner had abandoned his groceries and rushed from the shop. After a twenty-yard pursuit he'd rugby-tackled his faithful hound and brought it to a halt, whereupon the bin had rolled on top of him; and an elderly lady, suspecting him of animal cruelty, had belaboured his head with her umbrella. The cat, which had jumped on top of a wall to escape the dog's attentions, had watched the drama unfold with paw-licking nonchalance.

The flash of Gabriella's camera distracted both St Jerome and Moses. They thought it was lightning signifying Divine Wrath, for in her anorak and hood Gabriella resembled a Heavenly Messenger. However, they didn't bow down before her: St Jerome suffered from osteoarthritis and Moses wasn't the kneeling type, especially in wet weather.

Gabriella asked: 'Do you two have any idea where and when you are?'

The reply was a brace of blank stares. She repeated the question in Latin and waited for St Jerome to translate it into Hebrew for the benefit of his antagonist.

'Not a bloody clue,' said St Jerome. His Latin was impeccable.

'You're beside the Boundary Stone separating the parishes of Eyam and Stoney Middleton in Derbyshire, England. Okay, make that Britannia. It's about 1750 years since you finished your Latin version of the Bible, and the chap you're talking to really *is* Moses. You made a pig's ear of translating the Hebrew for "beams of light". The word did *not* mean "horns".'

'Oh,' said St Jerome. 'No wonder he seems a bit put out. I thought he'd dropped one of those two lumps of stone on his foot and blamed me for it. Are you *sure* he's not supposed to have horns?'

Moses wrung out his beard and looked puzzled. Latin hadn't been invented in his day. Providence had once been benevolent.

'Just think yourself lucky he hasn't seen those Renaissance paintings that portray him with horns,' said Gabriella. 'They *were* your fault. If he finds out about them I hate to think what he might do with those two lumps of stone.'

Gabriella awoke again, wondering how Herr Dr von Tür would interpret this latest confection from dreamland. It seemed odd, even by dream standards, because she'd never been to Derbyshire. No one searches for her True Self in Derbyshire.

$\sim$

The man with two pseudonyms

Cuthbert awoke to find sunlight enlivening the spare blanket he'd used to hide the wardrobe door. A tenor voice sang in the garden, the melody modal and tedious, the words indiscernible, the rhythm picked out by a clicking of shears. A blackbird improvised a disgruntled descant. Cuthbert put on his clothes and industrial helmet, opened the door, tripped, and fell on his nose beside the stone mushroom. The tenor voice and shears fell silent. The blackbird sang on.

Then the shears and the tenor voice resumed. Hearing the sound of Cuthbert's plummet, the owner of the voice had looked towards the door of the cottage, seen nothing and no one, shrugged, and resumed his activities. Then Cuthbert struggled to his feet and groaned. The owner of the voice looked towards the cottage again, blinked, and at last noticed the new resident.

'Good morning,' he said.

'Gd mrning,' said Cuthbert, rubbing his nose. 'I spose yr de garner.'

'Your speech is orthographically economical. I congratulate you. Yes, it's my task to maintain the grounds, and also the fabric of the cottage. Is the food supply holding out?'

'Nt vry well. Need shopn.'

'I'll deal with that, sir. Please call me either Gardner or Carpenter, whichever you prefer. I use both pseudonyms.'

Cuthbert straightened his industrial helmet and blew his

nose. The nose remained sore but normal English phoneme service was restored.

'Do you have a real name? I'm Cuthbert Fell.'

'That explains it. Yes, I have a real name, but it's Ruritanian so no one can pronounce it. Including me.'

Cuthbert stared in the direction of the well, counted the butterflies on the nearest buddleia and pondered. He found the blackbird's descant soothing, albeit disgruntled.

'There's no such country as Ruritania. So you come from a place that doesn't exist.'

'I know. It's a handicap. I had to leave Ruritania when the authorities discovered my hobby. So I gave up being a serial killer, moved to England, and after a period of transition I took to stealing handbags instead. When a woman's handbag is taken from her it robs her of her True Self as well as her credit cards and other personal items. It's less messy than killing her but just as effective at terminating her earthly existence. I settled in Sniggerswick for a while, and later I followed the disgruntled blackbird south to Rotting Bishop. I moved in here. My former pastime is now remembered only in song.'

~

A SERIAL KILLER'S LAMENT

When I was young and in my prime
A maiden I did meet,
A maiden wan and woebegone
With pimples on her feet;
But in that merry month of May
When love they say is true,
The little lambs that skip and play
Will soon be mutton stew.

I took her by the cold white hand,
That maiden sad and pale,
And led her to a mossy bank
In a quiet sheltered dale.
'Twas there I took my felling axe
And neatly sliced her through;
That maiden once was pale and wan
But now she's pale and two.

'There are more verses,' said Gardner-Carpenter, 'but the excerpt should suffice. Rest in pieces.'

Cuthbert nodded. 'I'm glad you changed your hobby.'

'In retrospect, so am I. The change wasn't immediate, though; as I said, I went through a transitional phase. But necrophilia proved unsatisfying so I graduated to handbag theft.'

Cuthbert envied Gardner-Carpenter his life history. People with initiative always *moved on*, he thought. *Changed.* Tried new ventures. *Graduated.* Opportunities passed through Cuthbert like neutrinos, never interacting with him. Abdul had been pleased with this simile; Cuthbert had been nettled by it but admitted that Abdul had a point, as always. Cuthbert seemed unable to seize any of the chances that life presented to him. Nevertheless, when he recalled the dream of the falling star and his discovery of the hidden cottage, he wondered whether he might yet change, become victorious in his – as Abdul would call it – internal jihad.

'If you don't mind my asking,' said Cuthbert, 'what do you do with the handbags you steal?'

'I keep them in my sitting room. I have display cabinets full of them.' Gardner-Carpenter inspected his shears. 'I'll have to buy another display cabinet soon. Maybe another sitting room. What shopping do you need, Mr Fell?'

Cuthbert requested milk, cocoa and some sort of food. 'I've no money but I'll say thank you. Er … how long did your necrophilia phase last?'

'Only a few months,' said Gardner-Carpenter. Then he saw the cat, which was staring at them from beneath an azalea, its back to the ash tree and the well. He dropped his shears. 'Grzgrtskya!' he cried. 'Ubyazi ventu dar flkn fyelliski?' He blushed and added: 'Pardon my French. I'll do your shopping immediately, Mr Fell.'

The cat didn't move.

~

SONG OF A NECROPHILIAC

Now every night I'm holding tight
A maid that's truly mine;
Her limbs are smooth and pure and white
And in the moonbeams shine.
For an hour I've whispered in her ear
But she's never once replied –
Which is really not surprising, for
It's five weeks since she died.

I strangled her one starry eve
And hid her in the ground,
So though each night I hold her tight
She never makes a sound.
With many a burning kiss that night
I lovingly entombed her,
And still with passion burning bright
I lovingly exhume her.

And though her manner always seems
So distant, stiff and cold,
And the only makeup on her face
Is a greenish growth of mould,
The aromas that she now emits
No perfume emulates,
So I'll hold her tightly every night
'Til she disintegrates.

~

52

Remembrance Sunday, happy gnome, covert surveillance

Gabriella was recovering, but she was still too weak to recount the quest for her True Self. To pass the time, she asked Selina for *her* life story.

'I met your True Self in Bali while I was looking for mine, Selina. Your life story might help me to understand the encounter.'

'To tell my life story would take a lifetime. I can tell you some of it, I suppose. But about my True Self – what's she called? What is she like? What does she do? Is she married? Why was she in Bali?'

Gabriella said that Selina's True Self was called Aniles, and she was young and elegant and gorgeous and seemed to spend all her time on the beach looking beautiful, and she was in Bali because Bali is famous for beaches on which people can spend as much time as they like looking beautiful. But she didn't seem to be married.

'Oh,' said Selina. 'Well, no doubt her life story is more interesting than mine. Is there any particular part of my boring life you'd like to hear about?'

Gabriella closed her eyes and pondered.

'How did you strike up a friendship with your garden gnome?' she said.

'Ah. That happened years ago. After I'd been dumped at the altar, the security service recruited me because I was a champion athlete and I hated men.'

Gabriella considered the logic of this.

'In what way did the security service cause you to befriend a garden gnome?'

Selina went to the window and stared out at her past. The summer light burnished her skeletal figure.

'It happened on a Remembrance Sunday. A phone call woke me before dawn.'

◆

'Grmumph. Whssit?'

The digital clock was legible to the bleariest eye: half past six. But wasn't today *Sunday*?

'Good morning to you, too, Selina. Rise and shine. There's a job for you.'

'Bussi*suny*! Whajob?'

The voice from HQ explained the emergency in punctilious RP. (The G9s at HQ always spoke RP and conveyed their BS in quasi-acronyms – initials, in other words – the SOBs.) The G9's report shocked Selina into action: she was sitting bolt upright in bed in a matter of minutes.

'Oh, come on. It's the eleventh of November, not the first of April. Do you think I'm going to …? Oh. Oh, I see. Right. Okay, I'm on my way. More or less.'

Selina stumbled into the bathroom, where the light wasn't working, and then to her wardrobe, the darkness within which was impenetrable. Ignoring the yellow eyes and dripping mandibles she selected gear that would make her look like an MI5 officer in disguise rather than an MI5 officer not in disguise, though she eschewed the false moustache and monocle.

◆

He – the gender wasn't ostensive, apart from the beard, but it was generic – took the surname of the householder whose garden he inhabited. His forename signified the unbreakable rictus of his simulated facial muscles. The combination was unfortunate; given the choice he wouldn't have called himself Smiley Shufflebottom. Nevertheless there was always much to be grateful for, much to make a chap happy; and from red pointy hat to blue thigh-length boots, Smiley was happy. He couldn't stop smiling around the stem of his pipe, his little white beard bristling with merriment over his bright red jacket, especially when he pondered the unspoken thoughts of Mr Shufflebottom. If he'd had a chuckle muscle as well as a beard and a pipe and a pointy hat he'd never have stopped chuckling. As it was, he was happy to sit in the garden on a large plastic replica of the fruiting body of *Amonita muscaris*, watching seasons, neighbours, traffic and wildlife pass by the fence, staring in unending delight at clouds and sunshine, moon and stars, rain and snow, and waiting in cheerful patience for Mrs Shufflebottom to wash the bird crap and dog piss off him. Notwithstanding Mr Shufflebottom's wishes, Mrs Shufflebottom never wore thigh-length boots like Smiley's (albeit black and preferably of leather; PVC at a pinch). She was more likely to appear in carpet slippers and curlers, carrying a bucket and cloth.

But today was Remembrance Sunday and there was work to do. Chaps had responsibilities. Smiley rose from his *Amonita*, stretched, washed his face in the bird bath (no easy task since he couldn't take the pipe out of his mouth), and checked the time on the sundial. This had to wait until a convenient shaft of light struggled through a gap in the clouds, but there was no need to rush. If he set off at a leisurely pace, keeping out of sight of persons of nervous disposition, he'd be there in plenty of time.

◆

They were rooted in two traditions, Selina observed: Greek and Norse. The Greek root was the intellectual one. Its basis was γνωσις, meaning knowledge; whence γνωμη, meaning opinion or maxim. The "gnomon" of a sundial came from the same root; literally, a γνωμον was a carpenter's square. Selina supposed it had something to do with the Classical Greek obsession with geometry and right angles, though it stretched the post-Hellenistic imagination to connect knowledge with maxims, sundials, carpenter's squares and gnomes. And how many people knew the alternative definition of "gnome" – *a sententious encapsulation of a moral precept, usually in verse*? No wonder those little plastic buggers in suburban gardens grinned all the time.

But it was the Norse root that plumbed the darkness inherent in those chthonic creatures, revealing them as traditional guardians of the inner parts of the Earth and its treasures. The unwary should never trifle with them. As far as

Selina could recall, the word "gnome" to denote these dark beings of the North had appeared first in sixteenth century Latin documents attributed to Paracelsus. Even Paracelsus hadn't been able to contrive a way of writing "dwarf" in Latin. Nevertheless, her pre-dawn phone conversation had revealed a fusion of the Greek and Norse roots that had generated a philological and ontological banyan: those dark sprites with dark powers guarding dark places were also repositories of knowledge, sententious maxims and carpenters' squares.

Selina stuffed her electronic fount of wisdom into her faux-leather government-issue handbag and made her way towards the town square War Memorial, taking care not to look purposeful.

◆

It was a chilly day of celebratory solemnity, marching feet, uniforms and medals, speeches and brass bands, wreaths of poppies. Crowds converged on the War Memorial and brought the town centre to a standstill. Scarves around their ears, hands in pockets, they waited for the sundials to strike eleven. But scuttling unseen under hedges and fences, crawling through drainpipes and perching on the bumpers of unsuspecting vehicles, the town's plastic gnomes were heading the same way. They bore plastic garden implements, plastic fishing rods and hard pointy plastic hats. The Gnome Guard was on the march.

Selina's trained eyes, no longer bleary, spotted surreptitious movements as she made her way among the semi-detached gardens of suburbia. How many were there? The G9 and the other SOBs at HQ hadn't exaggerated; indeed, they might have underestimated. Making sure she wasn't overheard, she took out her phone and summoned backup.

◆

As she passed the front gate of 27 Montbretia Avenue she caught her first clear sight of one of the plastic menaces. He was sneaking along in the shadows of privet and laurel hedges, heading as anticipated towards the town centre. Pre-emptive action was called for. She dashed forward and seized the gnome by a blue thigh-length boot.

'Oy! Call that covert surveillance?' protested her captive.

'No, I call it nicking a troublemaker. I want a word.'

'Okay. "Antidisestablishmentarianism." No? All right, how about "taghairm"? Or "sooterkin"? Or "cablish"? Look them up on your electronic fount of wisdom. You'll be surprised.'

Selina tucked the gnome under her left arm and sought the nearest open cafe, keeping her government-issue handbag out of his reach. She didn't suppose plastic gnomes drank coffee, but she needed a cup.

◆

'I'm Selina Crumpett,' she said, swallowing the life-restoring beverage. 'What's your name?'

'Smiley Shufflebottom. I suppose neither of us is to blame.'

Selina drank more coffee. Smiley sat across the table from

her, pointy hat on head, smile on face, pipe in smile, white beard perky over red jacket. The staff and the other customers noticed nothing unusual; it was Sunday morning. Selina decided she liked Smiley. Coffee and a happy gnome brightened the day. However, she had work to do. He must be interrogated.

'We have intelligence–'

'Intelligence? Come on, Selina Crumpett. Could anyone mistake you for anything but an MI5 officer in disguise?'

'–that all gnomes in the area are planning a mass gathering to disrupt the Remembrance Day ceremony at the War Memorial. What do you know about this?'

Smiley would have shrugged if he could.

'Our contribution to national security has been ignored for too long. For years uncounted we've guarded you against things hidden beneath the Earth, particularly during times of war. Can you imagine what might crawl, ooze, slither and scuttle from the depths if we didn't?'

Selina couldn't, though her former fiancé had written stories about things that crawled, oozed, slithered and scuttled from the depths. The stories had been published in magazines with lurid covers and most of them were grammatically challenged.

'You can protest peacefully, Smiley. It's legal.'

Smiley's beard gave a dismissive wobble.

'Not effective. Today will bring to public notice our long-overdue right to be represented in national ceremonies. Our action will give us the headlines we deserve, the respect we merit.'

'Tell me what you've planned.'

'The details are secret, Selina. But I'll give you a couple of hints. Imagine the noise a euphonium makes when a gnome jumps into it, pointy hat first, while a big chap with a red face blows through the other end. And if someone bends over to lay a wreath of poppies and a gnome brandishing a fishing rod–'

'No, I'm *not* going to say "point taken".' Selina set down her empty cup and leaned forwards. 'Okay. I've called for backup. It will include a tanker full of a solvent that dissolves plastic, fitted with a hose pipe and accompanied by an operator who knows how to use it.'

Smiley almost lost his smile.

'That isn't nice. But all right, it puts a different complexion on things. I need to talk to our gnominated leaders. May I borrow your phone? Mine doesn't work. It's just a bit of plastic.'

◆

Selina received a commendation for her key role in preventing the gnome revolt, but the demands of the gnomes were duly recorded. The recorded demands were filed in a grey metal filing cabinet in an office lined with tongue and groove wood and institutional paint and grimy windows. Anyone who ventured into that office was beset by an assistant manager who demanded a critique of his abstract paintings.

But Smiley and Selina had established a rapport. At the gnome's behest she purchased him from the Shufflebottoms and ensconced him in her flat on a large pot bearing a rubber plant. During the evenings they conversed about etymology, mythology, dark forces, carpenters' squares and the nature of time, especially after a few drinks.

Mr Shufflebottom spent the proceeds from the sale of Smiley on a pair of black leather thigh-length boots for Mrs Shufflebottom. She wore them with her curlers, which spoiled the effect. It was ironic, he reflected, that the gnome who'd formerly inhabited his garden was now called Smiley Crumpett.

◆

'And when I moved here and bought Forlorn House,' said Selina, 'Smiley came with me. We'd be lost without each other now. He alerts me to visitors, I wash him regularly and I never wear carpet slippers and curlers.'

Then from the garden came a gnomic howl: '*Selina! Some dumb bum's let the Cat of Doom out of the bag!*'

Big Vince and the mangy dogs

Big Vince parked his Aston Martin where everyone could see it. Carrying his mandolin, he lumbered across the pavement to an alcohol-free pub called *The Jolly Jihadi*, which bore a black inn-sign on which white Arabic letters were inscribed.

'Good morning, infidel.' The barman was dressed from head to toe in black and his face was masked. 'What can I get for you?'

'Och, jist gie's a pint o' sherbet, mate,' said Big Vince.

There was a selection of fruit juices for sale, and there were packets of crisps; most flavours except smoky bacon. On the bar-top were bags of salted peanuts and goat scratchings. Posters advertised evening classes – IED Making for Beginners, Beheading Exercises for the Over-Fifties – and comedy shows by touring imams. Second-hand AK47s were available; phone this number. A few regulars sat around the tables exchanging gossip and admiring each other's explosive belts. ('Does my bomb look big in this?')

'I'm wonderin',' said Big Vince to the barman, 'if ye could mebbe help me oot. I'm lookin' fer a gadge ca'ed Cuthbert Fell. Traced him tae this toon, lost the trail. Anybody here ken whaur he is?'

The barman made a head movement and then shouted: 'al-Fie! Infidel here asking for the infidel called Cuthbert Fell.'

al-Fie rose from his chair, walked over to Big Vince and said, 'Perhaps I can help.' He too was dressed from head to toe in black and his face was masked. 'What's your business with Cuthbert Fell, may I ask?'

'Owes money, hasnae paid. He's needin' the shit kicked oot o' him.'

al-Fie nodded. 'In that case I'll be glad to help, but perhaps you'll be kind enough to do something for us in return.'

'Mebbe. Depends whit it is, like.'

al-Fie studied Big Vince and nodded again. He went into a back room and re-emerged from the darkness carrying a black leather case with a disturbing label.

'Cuthbert Fell was seen yesterday leaving town in a canary-yellow car with a woman's hat on the passenger seat,' he said. 'He was heading towards Mangy Dog Farm. The mangy dogs know the whereabouts of everyone who passes their gate.'

'Right. Cheers, mate.' Big Vince pointed at the case. 'Whit's in it, like?'

'I can't divulge that, but pray rest assured it isn't illegal. And don't worry, it won't explode.'

'I'm no' worried. Jist curious.'

'Please don't be curious. We'd like you to take the case and give it to someone. You'll find it impossible to open or break, and it's opaque to X-rays. The task we ask you to undertake is simple but it's very important. At risk of sounding melodramatic, one might almost say it's crucial for the world's future.'

Big Vince remained dubious.

'Sounds a wee bit dodgy, like.' He glanced around the room. The gossiping had ceased and all the masked faces were staring at him: al-Fie, al-Bert, al-Gernon, al-Exander, al-An.

'Aye, nae bother, mate, I'll tak it. Bit why me? And who're ye wantin' me to gie it tae, like, and where?'

'The mission won't take you far out of your way. We believe the woman to whom the case must be delivered is staying at Forlorn House, which isn't far from Mangy Dog Farm. She's an infidel, too. Her name is Gabriella de Clare. She's searching for her True Self. It's vital that she find it.'

al-Fie lifted the case towards Big Vince. Big Vince took it. It wasn't heavy. He gave it a surreptitious shake. Something metallic moved inside.

'Cannae beat findin' yer True Self,' said Big Vince. 'Went oot lookin' fer mine a few years back. Found a wise gadge wi' a long white beard whit lived at the top o' this mountain. Did loads o' meditation exercises wi' him. Took a wee while, but in the end I discovered ma True Self and learned ma true vocation, namely, kickin' the shit oot o' folk whit owes money.'

Approval murmured behind the array of black masks.

'Tell me, infidel,' said the barman, 'why didn't you go to an inn where *alcohol* can be bought? All infidels drink alcohol, don't they?'

'This yin disnae,' said Big Vince. 'I'm aye tryin' tae warn folk aboot the evils o' drink, having suffered a few sair heids in ma time. Made up a wee song aboot it.'

He tuned his mandolin.

～

BIG VINCE'S ANTI-DRINKING SONG

I beg you to think as you take that drink
To soften up your brain
How your guts will rebel and you'll feel like hell
And the drink will appear again.
Oh, heed my warning, you'll feel in the morning
Like the world at the Trump of Doom,
And your drink will be seen, still steaming and green,
In the middle of the room.

Consider the sorrow you'll suffer tomorrow
When your head has split in two:
With a mouth full of flies and fire in your eyes,
You'll think your days are through.
Though your heart is still beating, you won't fancy eating,
Your flesh will be all a-quiver.
It will soon be too late to contemplate
Cirrhosis of the liver.

The Aston Martin picked its way along the track. Big Vince heard Mangy Dog Farm before he could see it; the canine voices were chanting the Mangy Dog Talking Blues in a disharmonious caricature of unison. At the gate he was accorded polite greetings.

'Polite greetings. I'm Mangy Dog One, pack leader.'

'Pleased tae mak yer acquaintance. I'm Big Vince o' the Merchant & Grendel Enforcement Agency. I'm wantin' tae find a gadge ca'ed Cuthbert Fell so I can kick the shit oot o' him.'

Mangy Dog One urinated on a cotoneaster.

'Cuthbert Fell? Canary yellow Volkswagen? Woman's hat on the passenger seat? He passed here yesterday. Sniffer Simon will track him for you when he's back from the fields. Care for some lunch? Sam and Ella are busy in the kitchen.'

From somewhere behind the farmhouse a mangy dog was howling.

'That's no' Sniffer Simon makin' yon racket, is it?'

'Good heavens no, that's Jerry Mire, otherwise known as Grimpen. Wallows in swamps. Most of us think he's a dead loss but in truth he's a live prophet. He's gifted with second smell.'

Lunch was *fillet de corbeau pourri* with a side dish of bone au gratin, accompanied by a rare 1997 Romney Marsh ditchwater. Sam and Ella had excelled themselves. Big Vince declared the repast was like tae gar him boak.

'Feel free,' said Mangy Dog One, wolfing down his *corbeau*. 'The bone is home-grown. Excellent crop last autumn. And my bitch caught the crow herself. That not right, MD Two?'

The bitch simpered halitotically and scratched her fleas,

which hopped around her mangy fur in time to her choice of music.

'Want any more before the pack gets back from bone-planting?' she asked.

'I dinna think sae,' said Big Vince. 'Like I said, it gies me the green boak.'

'I'll pass your on compliment to the chefs. Do you like the spring flowers?'

The bitch gestured towards a Ming vase of dead daffodils and a minging vase of crumbling crocuses.

'Mebbe no' jist at their best, but aye.'

'Our puppy put them there because he hates them and likes to see them dead. Hey, MD Three! Oh, no, he's rolling in his lunch again. Deal with him, MD One.'

Mangy Dog One chastised his offspring, licked him clean and ordered him to recite a poem in praise of spring flowers. The puppy complied with mangy alacrity.

~

DAFFODILS: A DOG'S PERSPECTIVE

I bounced out in the April breeze
That blows the scents across the hills,
And there beneath the sodding trees
Were all these sodding daffodils;
Upon the grass they sag and sway
And get right in a puppy's way.

They grew, I saw at single glance,
So dense and variously angled
Their nodding heads and sprightly dance
Would get a hapless canine tangled;
I peer through 'prisoning flowers and shoots –
The silly humans think it's cute.

So now when on my back I lie
And wag my tail from side to side,
They flash upon that inward eye
And make my grin grow very wide;
And then with joy my bladder fills
And pisses on the daffodils.

~

Big Vince loved the pastoral style of the early nineteenth century English romantic poets.

'No' as guid as oor Rabbie, but no' bad fer Sassenachs. An' yon poem o' MD3's is right oot o' Keats or Shelley or one o' that crowd. Like a wee verse I wrote aboot boakin' whin I used tae drink:

'Oh boak, green boak, that splasheth on my shoes,
 'Thou dismal aftermath of surplus booze!
 'As I behold each sev'ral splatter'd shoe,
  'A melancholy sense of *déjà bu*
 'Enshrouds my soul; for when night's hours I soak,
 'How green the morning face, how green the boak!'

The applause that greeted Big Vince's recitation was interrupted by a despairing cry from Jerry Mire.

'Woooooooooooooooooooooooeeeeeeeeeeeeeeeeeeee! Wooooooooooooeeeeeeeeeeee! The Cat of Doom hath been let out of the bag!'

'Oh, no. You're kidding!' said Mangy Dog One. 'How did you find out?'

Jerry Mire looked shifty. And mangy.

'Don't spread it around,' he whispered, 'but a gnome told me.'

Mangy Dog One heaved a sigh. Big Vince heaved.

'Must be true, then,' said Mangy Dog One. 'Who let the Cat of Doom out of its bag?'

'According to the gnome, a dumb bum.' Jerry thrust his muzzle to the sky and howled again. 'Big Vince, thou art too late!'

'Och, we'll see aboot that,' said Big Vince. He grinned at the puppy, Mangy Dog Three. 'Got any mair o' yer wee poems, then?'

Mangy Dog Three looked as embarrassed as a mangy puppy-dog can. His mother, Mangy Dog Two, explained about the sheepskin rug.

'He likes to lie on it, but ever since we told him the fairy story about the princess and the pea he's been fussy about sharing it. He once found a dead bluebottle on it and wouldn't lie down again until his father had eaten the offending insect. Then he made up a little song.'

The puppy was persuaded to sing his dead bluebottle song provided Big Vince agreed to accompany him on the mandolin. Big Vince went to his Aston Martin and collected the instrument.

~

SHEEPSKIN RUG LAMENT

There's an old dead bug
On my sheepskin rug,
Which is not a thing I'd care to lie on,
For a sheepskin rug
Is warm and snug,
But I don't want one that's got an old dead fly on.
A nice soft fleece
Is guaranteed to please,
But old dead flies just cause disease,
So if you want this dog
To be safe and snug,
Then come and get that old dead bug off my sheepskin rug.

~

Tree talk

While Big Vince conversed with the mangy dogs, Winston the white poplar grew thoughtful. Proclamations and commands from Yggdrasilsdottir often affected him that way.

'You know, Esmerelda,' he said, 'animals are inside out and inflexible. They're not like us.'

Esmerelda didn't understand. Winston explained: animals have their respiratory and digestive systems on the inside, and if you try to take them out, the animals object loudly and then die. They can't go into states of suspended vegetation through the winter, and their respiratory and digestive organs don't re-grow in the spring as a tree's do.

A memory of autumn whispered through Esmerelda's leaves. She remembered gazing downwards a few months ago, bent by a south-easterly, her berries blushing as she surveyed the drifts of golden clichés where her respiratory and digestive organs had fallen. She shook her twigs.

'Animals aren't inflexible, Winston. They bend better than us. Except armadillos and tortoises.'

'I meant inflexible in the metaphorical sense. If our respiratory and digestive systems were on the inside, they wouldn't work.'

Winston was right, thought Esmerelda. She wondered how animals contrived to breathe and eat when all their physiologically essential bits were hidden under their barks.

'But some of them *do* switch off for winter, like us,' she said.

'Hedgehogs. You know, those things like little hawthorn shrubs that move around. They stop working until spring.'

'They don't drop their respiratory and digestive systems on the ground, though,' said Winston.

The two trees lapsed into silent reverie. Standing between them, Smiley the gnome looked long-suffering, notwithstanding his merry smile. Then came the giant ash tree's judgment.

'You speak wisely, White Poplar. But it is not only the respiratory and digestive organs of animals that remain hidden yet functional. Humans, whose numbers have made them a worldwide plague, conceal their reproductive organs, too. Yet they reproduce more freely than the Earth can tolerate.'

'Indeed, Yggdrasilsdottir,' said Winston, 'it is a great paradox.'

'And as Jerry Mire would tell us,' added Yggdrasilsdottir, 'because of human fecundity, the end is nigh.' She paused, and then added: 'Nigher than the beginning, at any rate.'

~

Cuthbert and Gardner-Carpenter debate the origin of language

Over a cup of cocoa with Gardner-Carpenter, Cuthbert suggested that poetry was the original speech of mankind. It would have been more correct to say "humankind", retorted Gardner-Carpenter, but Cuthbert would still have been wrong. The original speech of humankind – mankind, at any rate – comprised a limited repertoire of grunts, embellished with facial expressions, gestures and postures.

'Even today,' continued Garner-Carpenter, 'this rudimentary mode of communication can be witnessed among human groups that gather in city streets under the darkness of broken lamps, or in public houses and football stadia. Whether these groups should be studied by anthropologists or ethologists is a moot point, but their vocalisations would resist linguistic analysis.'

Gardner-Carpenter, argued Cuthbert, was claiming only that the primitive *precursors* of language weren't (and aren't) poetic. That was indisputable. *His* claim, however, didn't refer to proto-language but to the earliest fully-formed human tongues. Those *were* poetry. Once again he was appropriating one of Abdul's ideas without admitting to the borrowing. But in doing so he was following tradition: Western European scholars had spent the first three centuries of the second millennium CE appropriating ideas from Muslims without admitting it.

'All the great tales of the earliest empires and city states,' said Cuthbert, 'all their statutes and stories and rules and rituals and practices and prophecies were told in poetry, and they were recorded as poetry once writing appeared. Prose was a late-comer.'

'I seem to recall, Mr Fell, that written records of agricultural production, military stores and building work were sporadic, sparse and unadorned, though they were sometimes embellished with stylised pictures drawn for the benefit of the illiterate. That's another relic of early civilisation reflected on the walls of modern cities. You do have a case, though: the first significant post-Milesian writer to use prose rather than poetry was Aristotle, and Aristotle isn't as memorable or quotable as his predecessors, in so far as their writings survive.'

Cuthbert agreed: Aristotle was admired for his peerless brilliance, but his writings were far less quotable than those of his teacher Plato.

'To put it simply,' he said, 'prose isn't as easy to memorise as poetry.'

'So before the invention of writing,' said Gardner-Carpenter, 'and for some time afterwards, any substantial narrative had to take the form of poetry. Otherwise it would have been forgotten and therefore lost. But to call poetry the *original* speech of humankind – the speech before language – overstates the case.' Gardner-Carpenter smiled. 'I once heard a quotation from a first year English student's exam answer: *"The English language began in 400 AD, but people must have had some means of communicating before that, even if it was only by means of grunts and gestures".'* He shook his head and the smile broadened. 'Bad luck Sophocles. Bad luck Virgil. Ah, the grunt that was Greece, the gesture that was Rome!'

Cuthbert considered the things that needed to be said but couldn't be conveyed in straightforward words, at least in any of the straightforward words he knew. Visual representation, poetic imagery, music, perhaps even dance were needed to communicate the otherwise incommunicable. As he reflected, he grew aware again of the scrutiny of the silent cat, which was always near him but never seemed to move.

'That cat,' he said, eschewing poetry and opting for prose, albeit with a suspicion of hyperbole and a hint of metonymy, 'is getting on my nerves.'

'Mine as well,' said Gardner-Carpenter. 'But what the hell, Mr Fell, what to do about it I needn't tell, since it's something you already know full well.'

Cuthbert pondered the something he knew full well. 'Ah,' he said, and went into the bedroom and unplugged the mysterious electronic pyramid.

The cat vanished, leaving not so much as a grin. But Cuthbert sensed it was still there, unseen but watching. Again he missed Abdul's reassuring presence and unpoetical common sense. Gardner-Carpenter was erudite and interesting but not reassuring. Cuthbert didn't expect Gardner-Carpenter to say whether he thought the cat had really gone.

Nevertheless, back on Mangy Dog Farm, Jerry Mire detected the change.

'Woooooooooooooooooooooooeeeeeeeeeeeeeeeeeeee! Wooooooooooeeeeeeeeeeee! The Cat of Doom hath been shoved back into its bag!'

Perhaps he was howling once again on the basis of information received from Smiley Crumpett.

$\sim$

A meeting of minds

Big Vince left his Aston Martin beside the gate of Mangy Dog Farm and Sniffer Simon guided him along the track towards the hidden cottage. *En route*, they passed Forlorn House.

'Here, Simon, is this no' the place yon Jihadi gadge tellt me to go, so I can gie this thing to this Gabriella de Clare lassie?' Big Vince hefted the case. It rattled again. 'Best see if she's at hame, eh no?'

Sniffer Simon had no objection; women, like vicars, were good to visit because they proffered tea and biscuits. So he and Big Vince opened the gate in the newly-repaired paling fence beside Winston and made their way up the drive to Forlorn House. Smiley announced their arrival: *'Selina! Visitors! Big tattooed bugger and a mangy dog!'* Big Vince voiced his intention to kick the shit out of the gnome, but before he could put this plan into practice the door opened and Selina emerged to greet them. Big Vince turned his back on Smiley and explained their business.

'Sniffer Simon here frae the farm is takin' me tae find a gadge I need tae find, but I need tae find a lassie ca'ed Gabriella de Clare, tae, so I can gie her this case, an' a wee bird telled me she's stayin' here. Is that right, Missus?'

'The wee bird,' said the disgruntled blackbird, 'was not me. Or even I.'

Selina wished to know more about the visitors. She particularly wished to know what the case contained.

'I dinnae ken, Missus.'

'Don't call me "Missus". You may call me Selina.'

A spasm of half-recognition crossed Big Vince's face, effecting no aesthetic improvement.

'Selina.' He frowned. 'Sorry, nae offence meant. Aye … Look, I dinnae ken whit's in the case but they telled me it's no' illegal and winnae blow up. Maks a metallic noise when ye shake the case but it's no' heavy.' He frowned again. 'Selina …'

'Yes?'

'Och, I'm dreamin'. Thought I kenned ye frae somewhere.'

'Well, I don't know *you*. And I've heard that line before.' Selina glanced at Sniffer Simon and wrinkled her nose; Sniffer Simon wagged, images of biscuit teasing his mind. 'Gabriella's in bed, still recovering from her biking accident.'

Big Vince said he was sorry to hear Ms de Clare had suffered an accident and was *ipso facto* indisposed. He sounded sincere. Would Selina please take the case, he asked, and give it to Ms de Clare when she felt better? His demeanour, and his deployment of a Latin phrase, surprised Selina into a smile. Politeness and a hint of erudition are established devices for defrosting women, and Big Vince had life experience.

'Would you like to come in? I'll see if Gabriella's awake. She might be well enough for a brief visit. And maybe you'd like tea and biscuits.'

Big Vince said, 'Aye, thanks, that'd be guid,' and Sniffer Simon wagged a force eight gale around his hindquarters. They went indoors to the sitting room, where the display cabinet caught Big Vince's eye: running gear, cups, medals.

'I *dae* ken ye! Selina Crumpett! Marathon winner four times over! Ye were brilliant!'

'Five,' said Selina, trying not to feel ten years younger. 'Yes, I was. Were you a runner, Mr …?'

'No' much ae one. Had a go but I'd niver 'ae matched you. Used tae drink. Nae good if ye want tae be an athlete. Gi'ed up. Swore off the booze whin I discovered ma True Self.'

Selina blinked and invited Big Vince to sit down. He managed to sit without sticking his piercings into the upholstery, but the armchair moaned. Sniffer Simon ate a biscuit.

'Coincidence,' said Selina. 'I believe Gabriella is also looking for her True Self. I understand she stumbled upon mine, or a Self purporting to be mine, when her quest took her to Bali.'

And yon Jihadi gadge believes Gabriella needs to *find* her True Self, recalled Big Vince.

'Aye. No' a bad idea if ye can dae it,' he said. 'Me, I'd niver hae found ma True Self if it hadnae been fir an auld gadge wi' a long white beard whit lives at the top o' the mountain. Got me daein' meditation an' stuff.'

According to Gabriella's delirious mumblings, thought Selina, she'd also consulted an old man with a long white beard who lived at the top of a mountain; probably a different old man and a different mountain, though. Nevertheless, this tattooed, shaven-headed and pierced Glaswegian with the mysterious leather case seemed to have something in common with Gabriella. He'd gratified Selina by recognising her as a champion marathon runner, but now, it appeared, he shared something important with her lodger, which felt like betrayal. She was accustomed to betrayals by men but it was annoying.

Big Vince finished his tea, belched and rubbed his nose with the back of his hand. Selina wondered why she hadn't worn something prettier. Maybe she still had some makeup, somewhere in the house. She went upstairs, leaving her visitor to follow.

Gabriella awoke when she heard the staircase grumbling under Big Vince's boots. She sat up in bed, stared at the visitor and did a double take.

'Good gracious. Professor McGrotty! You've changed. What brings you here?'

Big Vince proffered the case and stared at Gabriella, trying to compel recognition. She must have known him during his university days. Could he remember her? No. The hundreds of student faces that had passed before his eyes in lecture theatres and tutorial rooms were now a homogeneous blur. Bored by so many coincidences, Sniffer Simon curled up in mangy sleep on a Persian rug embellished with the so-called 'Paisley pattern', which symbolises the everlasting flame of Zoroastrianism. Not that Sniffer Simon was converted the worship of Ahura Mazda.

'Aye,' agreed Big Vince. 'I've changed. I'm here oan business. Brought this case fir ye, though.'

Gabriella looked at the case and frowned. What business had brought Professor McGrotty to East Sussex, where had he obtained the case, and why was he now delivering it to her? She'd dreamed about that case and its contents. She'd dreamed about it often. She'd shared the dreams with no one, not even Herr Dr von Tür. They were unsettling dreams.

'You seem to have a great many dreams, Gabriella,' said Selina.

'Weel, we aw hae dreams,' said Big Vince. 'Did ye dae history at Uni, Ms de Clare?'

'Just as a subsid. I read ASNAC.' Gabriella blinked. 'Sorry, Selina. Anglo-Saxon, Norse and Celtic. You won't remember me, Professor. My name was Gerda Ekberg in my student days. I changed it when I didn't get married.'

'I never have dreams,' said Selina. 'Not since I was a young girl, when I dreamed about the flying rabbit.'

Sniffer Simon slept on. Big Vince scratched his nose and pondered.

'Ekberg. Gerda Ekberg … Here, ye're no' the Gerda Ekberg whit discovered yon Norse saga fragment and translated it, are ye?'

'Yes. *Cludgehammersaga.* How gratifying of you to remember, Professor McGrotty!'

'Aye. An' the tale o' Eric the Swiver forbye. I remember that yin. Eric the Swiver, son o' Cnut the Dyslexic, an' his great battle wi' the Saxon warlord Baldwig the Bewildered. Grippin' stuff, aye, though it's no' whit ye'd call reliable history.'

'A story of unbridled Scandiknavery,' said Gabriella, 'encapsulating the spirit of Norse folklore. Like his father before him, Eric the Swiver was apt to confuse both speech and action, so he was noted for raping monasteries and for pillaging women and then burning them to the ground. According to the tale, he perished miserably at the age of seventy when owing to failing eyesight he mistook the front end of a wolf for the back end of a woman.'

'Perhaps, Gabriella,' said Selina, 'you might consider introducing us. Though it seems this gentleman has already recognised me; or rather, he's recognised memorabilia from my more memorable days.'

Gabriella said of course: this was Professor Vincent Tacitus McGrotty, eminent historian, author of the only biography of Alexander the Great to be written in Glasgow dialect and entitled *Big Eck*, and of numerous other scholarly monographs and papers. Big Vince said all that academic stuff was behind him; he'd resigned his university post after discovering his True Self. He and Gabriella fell into conversation about the value of bicycles in the search for one's True Self and soon found themselves discussing the old philosopher with the long white beard who lived at the top of the mountain.

Selina went downstairs and out into the garden to talk to Smiley.

∿

CLUDGEHAMMERSAGA:
AN EXCERPT TRANSLATED FROM OLD NORSE

Forth went Thorfinn, mighty Hammer of Cludge
With his score of iron-clad warriors –
Twenty consignments of canned muscle,
Brandishing spears fierce and fire-hardened.
They pulled the foam-flecked oars and sang the songs
For which their wives had banished them f
rom hearth and home,
And their longship harrowed the herrings' haven
As the mad mole marches through mulch.
Then yelled Thorfinn, mighty Hammer of Cludge,
'Oy, you lot, shut up and listen!
Behold, wrought by the hand of Baldur the bow-legged,
Cunning in artifice, famed fabricator of fine furnishings
By appointment to Odin, Chairman of the Board of Deities,
Who likes Valhalla to be comfortable,
I have here a pair of miniature longships,
Which even as you watch I fasten over my boots
With straps of reindeer hide steeped in tallow;
And taking in my hands this pair of antlers
Fixed to long ropes, which are secured to our ship's stern,
I step upon the water. Now, men, row fast,
Row harder than ever you have rowed,
Row till the ropes are taut and tight,
And I, mighty Hammer of Cludge,
Shall be Thorfinn Sea-Skimmer, Thorfinn Wave-Rider,
Thorfinn Cludgehammer, the world's first water-skier!'
Twenty oars rose and fell, a feeding frenzy on water,

Thrashing the whale-road, faster and faster
they clove the waves,
And Thorfinn laughed and roared,
and the longships on his feet
Pranced foam-prowed over the seal's path,
Until the crew, sea-weary, ceased their singing
And cried 'Sod this for a lark!'
With swords they sliced the ropes from the ship's stern
And rowed onward at gentler pace, pondering plunder;
But Thorfinn, dwindling into distance, cried
'You rotten lot! Come back! Just wait 'til I glug glug glug gl—'

~

The flying rabbit

'It was a strange dream,' said Selina. 'I don't think I ever told you about it.'

'Probably not,' said Smiley. 'In what way was it strange – in comparison, say, to other dreams?'

'The aftermath. I'd just started secondary school and I was staying with my uncle and aunt in Chipping Sodbury. I had the dream and then, in the morning, the parchment was lying there on my bed ...'

Selina frowned at the parchment, turned it upside down, and read it. Who was Regnarta?

'Uncle,' she asked, 'who's Regnarta?'

'No idea.'

Selina's uncle resumed his study of the morning tabloid. There was a column on page two about a werewolf in the Vale of Evesham. The photograph on the facing page was eye-catching but irrelevant.

'Aunt,' asked Selina, 'who's Regnarta?'

'Who, dear?' *Selina's aunt put down her dustpan and struck her husband's head with the back of the brush.* 'Alf, turn that page before the girl sees it. What were you asking, Selina?'

'See, Aunt, this parchment was lying on my bed when I woke up. The rabbit who'd brought it was leaping out of the window and flying away westwards so I didn't have time to ask her about it. But I'm sure rabbits don't write in Gothic script. Not even flying rabbits.'

Selina's uncle grunted and read the sports pages. They alternated with advertisements and there was a crossword. The crossword was a big white square with a little number "1" at the top left hand corner. The clues read: Across. 1, The indefinite article. Down. 1, The first letter of the alphabet.

'Let me see the parchment, pet.'

Selina handed the yellow document to her aunt, who polished her pince-nez and squinted at the dark red letters. She sniffed. The parchment emitted a musty aroma with a hint of incense, evoking a cathedral crypt. Her mouth set in a determined pucker.

'Selina, whoever this Regnata person is, you will not *meet him, her or it under the ash tree beside the crossroads at midnight after the next full moon has shone. Is that clear? Nor will you meet him, her or it anywhere else or at any other time unless he, she or it presents him, her or itself here at a respectable hour on a Sunday afternoon and explains his, her or its business over tea and biscuits in the parlour. Tell that to your flying rabbit. Alf, put that paper down and go and water the geraniums. You can tackle the crossword later.'*

'Gerania,' muttered Selina, sotto voce.

Smiley smiled around his pipe.

'Do you still have that parchment, Selina? And did you ever meet Regnata, or discover who Regnata was or is?'

'I never so much as heard of Regnata again. But I do still have the parchment, I think. Somewhere. Probably in the same place as my makeup box.'

'And did you ever discover why you dreamed about a flying rabbit?'

Selina shook her head. She'd visited a psychotherapist called Janua and asked her to explain it. The psychotherapist had told her the flying rabbit related to both her past and her future, and to come to terms with its meaning she would have to dress in canary yellow.

'So I dressed in canary yellow but it didn't help. I didn't go back to see Janua again.'

And then a long-forgotten memory circuit sparked. She knew where the parchment was, and where her makeup box was! They were in the bottom drawer of the chest of drawers in the guest bedroom currently occupied by Gabriella, together with a cornucopia of odds and ends such as a single sock and an unpaired cufflink.

A discourse on pyramids

'The etymological root of "pyramid" is "pyre",' said Gardner-Carpenter, 'so if you interfere with pyramids you're playing with fire. If you're into alchemical and mythological stuff you can interpret the fire as enlightenment, illumination, primal energy, the Creative Seed, the Divine Principle. But if you're not careful you're likely to burn your fingers and set your trousers alight.'

'Okay,' said Cuthbert, 'so what was Ancient Egyptian for "pyramid"? What did it mean to them?'

'Per-Neter, or Per-Neteru,' said Gardner-Carpenter. 'House of Divine Principles. The Divine Principles are the original Creative Seeds, the cosmic laws that give energy, purpose and expression to all things.'

'Not what you'd call scientific,' said Cuthbert, echoing Abdul's contempt for New Age eyewash. 'More like unadulterated bollocks. But the pyramid I had to switch off to get rid of the cat–'

'Is a device using modern electronics in a way no one understands. So what?'

Cuthbert envisaged the Primordial Mound arising in pyramid shape from the Waters of Chaos. He shook his head to dispel the image. His industrial helmet fell off.

'Look, Mr Fell, the Great Pyramids are made of four upwardly-pointing equilateral triangles meeting at a single point closest to the sky. Do you not agree?'

'To quote you,' said Cuthbert, retrieving the helmet. 'So what?'

'Sacred Geometry. The triangle has three sides. Three is the number of Creation. Four is the number of Destruction. The upwardly-pointing triangle is the alchemical symbol for Fire. And the Pyramid is built on solid bedrock.'

'Not the one I found in the wardrobe. It's got a wooden base.'

Gardner-Carpenter nodded as though a point had been proved.

'Yes. *Ash* wood.' He allowed half a minute for Cuthbert to grasp the significance of the observation. Cuthbert didn't. Then he continued: 'The base symbolises where the mass of humanity congregates, where the rat-race is run. Only a few humans have the spiritual awareness to ascend the sides to higher levels, even though the Pyramid is stepped.'

'The one in the wardrobe isn't stepped.'

'No? Look more carefully, Mr Fell. Also, unless you know how to navigate around the Pyramid, you can see only one face, one triangle, at a time. It is easier to appreciate the four-sided nature of the structure, to perceive the symbolic fusion of Creation with Destruction, when you climb to higher levels, away from the mass of humanity.'

Cuthbert shook his head, trying not to dislodge the industrial helmet again.

'And you gained this spiritual awareness through being a serial killer turned necrophiliac turned handbag thief turned carpenter and gardener?'

'You see what I mean by climbing to higher levels?'

Cuthbert recalled hearing that one function of pyramids was to transform metallic objects: aligned with the Earth's magnetic field, for example, a pyramid can sharpen dull razor blades. And Herr Dr von Tür had told him that the entrance to a pyramid seen in a dream signifies the quest for one's True Self, the integration of Self and Soul, of the Individual Consciousness with Universal Consciousness. Cuthbert had discussed both allegations at length with Abdul. They'd agreed that all claims about the powers and significance of pyramids were twenty-four carat horse shit.

'You might as well say that the triangular face represents the Holy Trinity,' he said, recalling Patricia the Anglican vicar.

'Exactly,' said Gardner-Carpenter. 'Where do you suppose the early Christians got the concept of the Trinity from?'

PYRAMIDS

Still stand the mighty Pyramids
Like fossilised scorpaenids;
No sign of serious decay
Threatens to wear them yet away,
For storms erode their stony hide
No faster than a mountainside,
And Time, who sandblasts all that pass,
Respects their pyramidal mass,
Devouring these too-solid ghosts
Slower than sea-waves scour the coasts;
Through several millennia
No fungus-grown hymenia
Have blemished their geometry.
Say, does their stereometry
Model our sociometry
As Gardner-Carpenter protests,
And does their mighty form attest
To Primal Urge and Heavenly Fire –
Or's Gardner-Carpenter a liar?
Isn't all this mystic stuff
A load of pestilential guff,
Since all those big old stony things
Were just sarcophagi for kings?
Surely they have no power at all
To sharpen razor blades, or call
Creative Seeds to germinate …
Yet to reject I hesitate
Because the one in Cuthbert's room
Can liberate the Cat of Doom.

Abstract art and a dream of four riders .

Emerging through the Georgian portico of the institution for the bewildered, suitcase in hand, Herr Dr von Tür met a large woman with a benevolent smile. This was no coincidence; the large woman with the benevolent smile was seeking him. She wore flat sandals, a flowery dress that resembled a cross between Sir Francis Dashwood's cloak and a bell-tent, and a hat in the form of a demoralised pancake decorated with an artificial pink rose and lacy bits. Her hair was grey and styled.

'Ah. You wish a consultation with me to make?'

'Oh, no, Doctor.' The large woman didn't titter. 'I've come to ensure your wellbeing, to guide your footsteps as you re-enter the everyday world. Shall we have a cup of tea?'

Herr Dr von Tür examined his polished shoes. He saw in them no need for guidance, only a reflection of the summer sky, partially obscured by a distorted image of his face.

'If we somewhere near at hand can a cup of tea become, we shall that cup of tea then enjoy. By "have", madam, you mean perhaps "drink"?'

The large woman made a mental note about precision. Herr Dr von Tür dusted his pince-nez and scrutinised his companion. She responded to the scrutiny with neither blush nor umbrage and led him to a nearby outdoor café.

The seats were impossible: either too high and insecure for the tables, or too low and narrow to accommodate the hindquarters of a human adult, especially those of a large woman in an expansive flowery dress. There was no hot water, so they went to the manager's office to ask for some. The office was poky, lit only by a small grimy window and lined with tongue-and-groove wood painted in the institutional colours now familiar to Herr Dr von Tür, who studied his companion through all-seeing professional lenses.

'You have previously this establishment visited, perhaps?' When she vouchsafed no answer, except to look about her with a mystified air, he continued: 'Anything here puzzles you, I think?'

She shook her head.

'No, I've never been here before. Yet it seems familiar. I knew what this office looked like before we entered. I'd even anticipated the lack of hot water.'

Herr Dr von Tür's face expressed delight, even triumph.

'Aha! So, it is *déjà vu* you experience, yes? You have often *déjà vu*?'

She shook her head again.

'Not since I was young and … I'm sorry, I didn't introduce myself. I'm Patricia. Or, if you prefer to be formal, the Rev. Patricia–'

'So! I must some questions ask and from your answers we shall this *déjà vu* experience begin to comprehend. Pray do not be alarmed. You have a sentence begun, "Not since I was young …", but this sentence you have not finished. First, then, we must without delay–'

The assistant manager appeared, provided them with hot water and tea bags, and invited them to examine his abstract paintings and offer a critique. Patricia had anticipated the request, though she knew not how or why. She gazed at a canvas entitled *This Way Up* and affirmed that she was no judge of art. The background hue of *This Way Up* faded from indigo at the top to cerulean blue at the bottom. One third of the way from the left, near the top of the painting, was an oval structure of brilliant red and yellow, an ellipse of fire. Two bands of colour proceeded downwards from the ellipse and returned to it, forming curved triangles or flattened inverted hearts with the ellipse at their apices: an intense yellow band that reached out towards the viewer, and a cadmium red one that retreated into the rear of the picture. Between them were two spheres, one large and deep purple, the other smaller and viridian green. If Patricia had been wearing Cuthbert's industrial helmet it would have fallen off with mystification. She sipped her tea.

Herr Dr von Tür interpreted *This Way Up* with the confidence only a psychotherapist can command.

'Aha! We the illusion of three dimensional space here experience, yet we know we can only two dimensions see. Triangles of coloured fire we observe, but the fire has those triangles softened so they curves not angles make, and their bases are not secure or rectilinear, and therefore they are female and hot. And between them are the male organs of reproduction entrapped, and those organs are cool. And their sizes are unequal, as I observe, so they a species of sexual imbalance manifest. Is it not so, sir?'

That isn't what I see in the painting, thought Patricia. The coloured shapes look a bit like alien spacecraft, or perhaps something symbolising … Oh, I don't know. It's quite pretty, though.

'I want to imagine two more of those coloured bands,' she said, 'both at right angles to the ones in the painting, all joining together at that oval apex. It's like a halo, that apex. Or a capstone.'

'Yeah, right,' said the assistant manager. 'Do you want another cuppa? And would you like to see some more paintings?'

They looked at three other paintings, each less comprehensible than the one before except to Herr Dr von Tür, who interpreted all of them. But the assistant manager was disappointed: the psychotherapist's expositions included no evaluation of artistic merit. Taking mild umbrage, he declined a pressing invitation to his visitor's consulting room where his sexual imbalance could be explored.

Patricia's eye was caught by a grey metal filing cabinet. She opened it, to the consternation of the assistant manager. She knew what she'd find inside it.

'I need to take charge of this,' she said, stuffing into her handbag the report on the Remembrance Sunday Gnome Revolt and the gnomes' demands.

As she left the office and walked into the spring sunshine beside Herr Dr von Tür, leaving the assistant manager's protests and paintings behind her, Patricia observed that the experience had verged upon weirdness.

'Perhaps so; perhaps not so.' The psychotherapist looked wise, though his beard was neither long nor white. 'That final painting has the memory of a former dream of mine evoked. Four horses with riders, from four different directions approaching, yet also side by side riding–'

'Oh yes,' said Patricia, 'the four riders. It's sure to happen some day, probably quite soon.'

Come to that, she thought, the entire café has a former dream of mine evoked. At least, I suppose it has. Otherwise, how would I have known the report was in that filing cabinet?

'But first, dear lady, we must your *déjà vu* experience explore. I beg you will my footsteps to my consulting room please guide.'

~

Gabriella resumes her quest

Stroking the leather case, Gabriella sensed the spiritual refreshment and elevation normally attained only through the purchase of a new handbag. She remained in bed but her eyes, her posture and the movements of her hands manifested a renewed urge to be up and doing.

'Are you any good at repairing bicycles, Professor?'

'Nut,' said Big Vince. 'Whit happened tae yours, like?'

Gabriella recounted the incident with the careless motorist and her collision with Winston and the paling fence.

'Drivers like yon,' said Big Vince,' are needin' the shit kicked oot of 'em.'

'Perhaps,' said Gabriella, her eyes full of distant horizons, if not other worlds, 'but there's a strong environmental argument in favour of reckless driving … Oh, well, it isn't a problem. I can walk.'

'Where tae, like?'

'The place where at last I'll find my True Self. I don't think it will be a long journey. I believe I was nearly there when the accident occurred; but nothing happens without a purpose. If it hadn't been for the accident I wouldn't have been holed up here in Forlorn House, so I wouldn't have received the case from you before I reached my destination.'

Gabriella's reasoning puzzled Big Vince, but he attributed his puzzlement to her gender. Also, he reflected, the fatalistic view of history, the belief that events in the world follow a

Plan, was never defensible: to the despair of his erstwhile Marxist colleagues and the Calvinist preachers in his Presbyterian Kirk, he espoused the Tolstoyan antithesis of predestination or historical inevitability. So he gave scant consideration to Gabriella's remarks.

'Aye, weel, we'll need to git goin' tae, me an' Sniffer Simon. If he's ever goin' tae wake up, that is. I need tae find this gadge ca'ed Cuthbert Fell and Simon's goin' tae lead me tae him. Right, Simon?'

Cuthbert Fell, thought Gabriella. Why does the name sound familiar? Her hands caressed the leather case again. It gave a metallic rattle, at once reassuring and unsettling, but the significance of Cuthbert's name eluded her. Sniffer Simon stood and stretched and his tail fanned her with a cool gale. It made her feel like the glade in a well-known aria from Handel's *Semele*.

'Where's Selina gone?' she wondered.

'Oot,' said Big Vince. 'But I think she's oan her way back in.' Divining Gabriella's wish to dress before she renewed her quest, he added, 'I'll nip doon the stair an' see whither I can help wi' onythin'.'

Once again his boots threatened the integrity of the staircase. Gabriella rose, went for a shower and dressed herself. Selina declined her visitor's offer of assistance. Her brusqueness was seasoned with waspishness.

'When did ye last go oot, Selina? Oot o' yer ain gairden, I mean?'

'When I last went shopping.'

'Shopping? That all? Och, ye live in countryside like this,

right on the coast, an' ye dinnae gae fir walks? Or even runs? Dinnae tell me ye havenae time. I mean, a marathon runner–'

'That was in the long-forgotten past. I got bunions.'

'Oh, right, I see. No' sae guid. Bad enough so ye cannae walk oot o' yer gairden, are they?'

'No, I got them operated on. I can walk. But what's the point? You walk somewhere, and all that happens afterwards is you return to where you started.'

'Aye, but it's no' the same as niver gaein' oot i' the first place. *Tae arrive back where we started and tae ken the place fir the first time.* Whae wrote that? Cannae mind.'

'Eliot. And when I do go out, I *don't* know Forlorn House any better when I return than I did when I left. No surprise there, surely? The Earth turns full circle every twenty-four hours or so and it doesn't seem to grow any wiser, nor does the passing of yet another year add a new layer of understanding to the planet. I reckon Eliot was talking through his arse.'

Big Vince wasn't sure that Eliot's poem was intended to be read literally but he elected not to argue. Instead, he described Gabriella's apparent recovery and her intention to set out again to her destination.

'Oh, I see,' said Selina. 'And I suppose you'll go with her.'

'Dinnae ken aboot that. I've my ain fish tae fry. Need to find this gadge ca'ed Cuthbert Fell an' kick the shit oot o' him, 'cos he owes money fir his rent an' he's rin away instead o' payin'.'

'Really. And does Gabriella know that?'

'Aye. Jist tellt her.'

'Did she not suffer a relapse when she learned that your way will diverge from hers? Your arrival exerted *such* a magical effect on her health. It would be sad if the restoration were undone.'

Big Vince explained it was Gabriella's receipt of the leather case, not his arrival, that had improved her condition. However, Selina wasn't disposed to listen to excuses. She was convinced that Big Vince intended to accompany Gabriella on her journey. Therefore, she decided she'd tag along, too. After all, he'd just urged her to take walks. But before she set out she went upstairs to the guest bedroom. There were items she needed to find. Gabriella stopped brushing her hair and smiled at her. Selina ignored the smile, went to the chest and opened the bottom drawer.

Yes! She was right! There was her old makeup box! And the parchment left by the flying rabbit! And the single sock, and the unpaired cufflink, and a box of crayons, the broken chessmen, the size thirteen shoe sole, and an assortment of other items that couldn't be construed as anything more than the sediment of everyman's life, and everywoman's.

~

ALL THAT WE ARE

In the end it's all we are,
Unimportant trivia,
Bits and pieces, bits and bobs,
Odds and ends and odds and sods,
Remnants, paraphernalia,
Snippets, knick-knacks, miscellanea,
Rubbish, litter, bric-a-brac,
Oddments, fragments, heaps of crap,
Flotsam and jetsam, cuttings, leavings –
Such remains don't merit grieving;
Debris and detritus too,
Sundries, scraps like me and you,
Clobber, gubbins, junk and stuff,
Leftovers – we're not enough;
Crummage and truck, they used to say,
Set aside for rainy day,
Offcuts, leftovers, costume blings:
We are all disposable things.

~

Smiley the Hegelian

Selina returned to the garden with Big Vince, who stared at Smiley and pondered, head tilted to one side. Smiley stared back, smiling around the stem of his pipe.

'Jist wondering, like,' said Big Vince, 'aboot gnomes. I mean, like, γνῶσις means knowledge, aye? And the auld Greeks derived γνώμη frae the self-same etymological root. So daes this gnome o' yours gie oot much i' the way of opinions an' maxims? I mean, forbye announcin' ma arrival here wi' Sniffer Simon as "Big tattooed bugger an' a mangy dog"?'

'You might consider asking the gnome directly, you big tattooed bugger,' said Smiley.

'If it wasnae likely tae upset Selina,' said Big Vince, 'I'd kick the shit oot o' ye here an' noo, ye wee plastic bastard.'

Selina said she too was puzzled by the semantic interconnections among knowledge, opinions, sundials and carpenters' squares, since γνώμον also sprung from the same etymological root. She'd discussed the matter many times with Smiley, even before they'd moved to Forlorn House, but her puzzlement remained. Thanks to the results of her recent bottom-drawer exploration, the puzzlement was now enhanced by mascara and blusher.

'Do you think it's anything to do with the Greek obsession with geometry, Professor McGrotty?'

'Jist ca' me Vince.' Big Vince inserted a little finger into his right ear and rotated it seven times. 'Dinnae ken, tae be honest,

Selina. An' I dinnae ken why the self-same word should denote a sententious encapsulation o' a moral precept, usually i' verse, like.'

He withdrew the finger from his ear and examined it. He found no enlightenment, only a quantity of wax and a small dead insect, possibly an *Acarus siro*.

'You don't understand because you're only looking at one facet of Gnomehood,' said Smiley. 'I believe Ms de Clare will be able to articulate the other. And that other facet seems likely to predominate in the foreseeable future.'

Silence descended upon the trio and reigned until Gabriella emerged from the house, scarcely limping, carrying her new handbag and the rattling leather case. Her arrival transformed the group of three to a group of four. She wore colourful feminine clothes and her hair was neat. Smiley blinked, but no one noticed except Winston and Esmerelda, who both kept their counsel; trees have their own slow rhythms, and Yggdrasilsdottir had forewarned them of the dramas that were about to unfold. Selina and Big Vince stared at Gabriella while Gabriella admired her reflection in the bird bath. The clouds that framed her image against the cerulean sky made her look as though she'd grown wings.

Selina unprimmed her mouth without perturbing the layer of lipstick.

'Can you articulate the other facet of gnomehood, Gabriella? The Norse perspective? I suppose it must fall within your sphere of expertise since you studied ASNAC and translated *Cludgehammersaga*, not to mention other ancient Norse lore, about which Professor McGrotty seemed inclined to rhapsodise.'

Gabriella told her that gnomes were guardians of the inner parts of the Earth and no one should trifle with them unless they were endowed with Certain Powers. 'Were it not for Smiley and his kindred, all sorts of unspeakabilia would emerge from the darkness beneath,' she said. She patted Smiley's red pointy plastic hat and winked at him.

'Och, aye. Paracelsus,' said Big Vince.

'So I'm told,' said Selina. 'But why are dark sprites with dark powers guarding dark places also repositories of knowledge, sententious maxims and carpenters' squares?'

'Why shouldn't we be?' said Smiley.

Selina and Big Vince looked puzzled. Sniffer Simon, who had at last woken and was now wandering to Big Vince's side, looked mangy.

'One can hardly guard dark places effectively unless one is a repository of knowledge,' said Gabriella. 'Isn't that so, Smiley?'

'An' mebbe ye need a few sententious maxims tae warn the unwary against messin' around wi' dark stuff, like,' said Big Vince.

'And I suppose the carpenter's square represents order,' said Selina, 'as opposed to chthonic chaos. So perhaps it's just a matter of balance.'

'Synthesis, more like,' said Smiley, 'between the thesis of order and the antithesis of disorder, the Greek tradition and the Norse. But there, you see, Selina: a little thought, a little discussion, and you've come at last to understand the philological banyan encapsulated in the word "gnome" that you and the rest of humankind attach to me and my kindred.'

He stared across the garden of Forlorn House and smiled.

⌒

On the nature of gardens

'And so,' said Cuthbert, 'after excelling as a handbag thief you became a gardener and a carpenter. What made you think those trades would ensure your ascent of the pyramid, if that's what you had in mind? And did you adopt your two pseudonyms to reflect your new trades, or did you choose the trades because you already had the pseudonyms?'

'Don't wander near the well,' said Gardner-Carpenter. 'It's bottomless, like William Pitt.'

'Elder or Younger?'

'Take your Pitt.' Gardner-Carpenter shrugged. 'Someone, I can't remember who, described working in an English garden as midway between throwing darts and composing sonnets. For those who know how and where to look, the garden is an encyclopaedia, an instruction manual for life; after all, as Francis Bacon reminded us, God created a Garden and put our earliest forebears into it. But perhaps Eve was more at home there than Adam because gardens aren't objects, they're processes, open-ended like all women's arts. Yet for all of us, male or female, gardening is pure creation and yields rewards and compensations out of all proportion to the gardener's efforts or the gardener's goals. It's the nearest thing a human can achieve to the Act of Creation.'

Cuthbert blew his nose, which was still sore from its encounter with the paving beside the stone mushroom.

'I'd have supposed gardening was a cascade of losses with

a few scraps of triumph borne on its all-destroying tide. As you say, pretty much like life. On the other hand, a garden is by definition land that's been tamed and civilised, not like wild Nature, which is outlaw country by comparison.'

Gardner-Carpenter said, 'Hmmm,' and looked at once enigmatic and contemplative, an accomplishment at which he excelled.

'What seems paradoxical, semantically speaking, is that all cognates of "garden" in French, German, Latin and most other Indo-European languages denote an enclosure, a closed-in space. And "closed-in space" is the literal definition, or translation, or characterisation, of Hell. Yet we associate gardens with Heaven.'

'Maybe Heaven is just another sort of closed-in space,' said Cuthbert.

'Plenty of literary and religious resonances, anyway,' said Gardner-Carpenter, 'and not only with the Garden of Eden. Have you read Hawthorne's *Rappaccini's Daughter*? Francis Hodgson Burnett's *The Secret Garden*?

'Had that one read to me when I was a child, but never heard of *Rappaccini's Daughter*.'

'*Roman de la Rose*? Or more to the point of our discussion, Berendt's *Midnight in the Garden of Good and Evil*?'

Cuthbert wondered why Berendt's dramatized tale of a murder in the American Deep South should be more to the point of their discussion. However, the only conclusion he could draw was that Gardner-Carpenter, despite his background and idiosyncratic pastimes, was a literatus. He'd heard about *Roman de la Rose* from Abdul, but hadn't read it;

Abdul, he reflected, was also a literatus. Then he fell to wondering whether "literatus" was a real word.

'I must catch up with my reading,' he said. 'But tell me, why do you say the well is bottomless?'

'Because it has no bottom,' said Gardner-Carpenter, 'which makes it useless for the purpose for which wells are normally dug, but potentially indispensable for chthonic unspeakabilia seeking egress into our world. You might have noticed the sulphurous aroma arising from it.'

Cuthbert had wondered about the sulphurous stench, but at that moment he was more exercised by the question of whether "unspeakabilium", like "literatus", was a proper English word, and why (if he recalled his Latin correctly) a denizen of the netherworld beneath the well should be grammatically neuter while a person of learning was masculine.

~

A Celtic knot

'This is intriguing,' said Patricia, perusing the file. 'The ways of God are convoluted, but we can see pleasing patterns in them – interconnections and symmetries – that recall the abstract paintings we were asked to examine and criticise at the café.'

Herr Dr von Tür adjusted his spectacles and rubbed his chin. His new patient's (or guide's) pronouncement must surely be related to her *déjà vu* experience, but at this stage in the consultation the connection was obscure. He asked her to speak more about the convoluted ways of God so that her underlying sexual imbalance could be diagnosed.

'During my teenage years–' she began.

'Aha!'

'–I was a Pagan and practised witchcraft. In those days I called myself Regnarta because I saw myself as someone alien to the bulk of humankind, but in reverse. Now and again I managed to transform myself into a flying rabbit, and it was in the guise of a flying rabbit that I visited a girl whose future I foresaw as interesting.'

'A flying rabbit. Yes, indeed. *Most* interesting. And this girl, what of her?'

'I left something on her bed while she slept: a parchment, written in blood in Gothic script. It asked her to meet me under the ash tree at the crossroads after the next full moon, a time I believed would be auspicious for divining her future in full technicolour detail. But leaving the parchment for her was a waste of time. She didn't come.'

Herr Dr von Tür nodded. This was a familiar pattern among patients with certain types of psychosexual imbalance. Typically, they became religious after they'd undergone a transforming experience.

'And since she has not come, what on you was then the effect?'

Patricia shrugged.

'Gave up witchcraft, converted from Paganism to Anglicanism, and never again metamorphosed into a flying rabbit. Though I still eat carrots and lettuce and dream about flying.'

Herr Dr von Tür invited her to continue.

'I knew the girl would achieve something,' said Patricia, 'so I followed her career, albeit from a distance. And indeed, events proved me right: she became a marathon runner, a five times champion; and then, as an MI5 operative, she was instrumental in suppressing the Remembrance Day Gnome Revolt. This …' She brandished the file from the grey metal filing cabinet. '… is the report of the gnomes' grievances and the promises they were given. Which of course were never fulfilled.'

Herr Dr von Tür still failed to see how this revelation related to the patient's *déjà vu*.

'That's the odd thing,' said Patricia. 'It was what I meant about the ways of God being convoluted and forming pleasing patterns. Several years ago I had a dream about that café and the assistant manager's abstract paintings. I'd never been there, but it was because of the dream that I recognised it today when we went for a cup of tea. In the dream I was accompanied by an acquaintance. He's a young man whom I don't much like because despite his intelligence he's an all-round failure.'

'And this intelligent young failure, he has perhaps a name?'

Patricia told Herr Dr von Tür the intelligent young failure's name and Herr Dr von Tür fell off his chair. Indeed, he thought, staring up at the ceiling, this new patient had displayed remarkable perception when she spoke of the convoluted patterns formed from the world's phenomena and *dramatis personae (et res)*. Follow any ribbon of events and personnel, he mused, and it will intertwine with others, bend back on itself, and lose you in the maze or labyrinth of interconnections it generates.

'Is it labyrinth or maze, this Celtic knot?' he wondered, still prostrate beside his chair.

Patricia bent over the prone psychotherapist, radiating concern.

'Are you all right, Doctor?'

'Perfectly. I can from this position a new perspective on these matters perceive. But now, what will you do this Celtic knot to disentangle, this dream and *déjà vu* experience to rationalise?'

'Follow the trail to its source. Find the girl, now a woman segueing from middle years to pensionable age.' Patricia shook her head. 'I wonder, in view of my vision, what catastrophe will unfold if she meets Cuthbert Fell ...'

In the eye of her imagination she saw the Four Riders as they'd appeared in the psychotherapist's dream.

∽

Towards the hidden cottage

'Och, it's no' as bad as that, Selina. Look on the bright side. Braw weather. Smell the sea air. An' Simon can smell mair than sea air, eh no, Simon?'

'Indeed, Big Vince,' said Sniffer Simon, 'the scent of the person out of whom you intend to kick the shit remains clear, though it's less strong now than it was a few days ago.'

Gabriella carried her new handbag over her shoulder and the leather case in her right hand. Her bicycle had served its purpose, she decided. It had brought her to within a hair's breadth of finding her True Self. Her eyes remained full of distant horizons and distant worlds. She was quiet.

'How does a dog contrive to follow the scent of someone who drove along the track in a car rather than walking?' said Selina. 'Especially a mangy dog?'

'My manginess is irrelevant,' said Sniffer Simon. 'The expert canine nose needs only a few volatile molecules from the target to determine direction. The lower parts of a car including the tyres are guaranteed to transfer enough aromatic components to the ground for tracking to be possible.'

'Aye. Jist sae long as ye find the wee rat, Simon. Come oan then, Selina, tell me a bit aboot yersel. I ken ye've been a great runner, an' an MI5 agent forebye, but whit else?'

Selina cast around for memories that Big Vince would find intriguing and possibly (who knew?) attractive.

'I used to spend hours every day,' she said, 'straightening

picture frames in my house, my neighbours' houses, hotels, restaurants, stately homes and art galleries. The Ministry hired a psychotherapist called von Tür to examine me. He told me I had OCD, which was nonsense, so I told him to piss off. After I quit MI5 I was offered a job at the Tate Modern as a cleaner, but the establishment drove me to drink because there was no way of telling whether the exhibits were straight or not, or even whether they were the right way up. So I handed in my notice and returned to my former life and happiness. Then I moved here.' She smiled. Few things, she decided, are more satisfying that concocting plausible but colourful lies and telling them in a convincing manner. 'What about you, Vince? I know you were a history professor, and then you discovered your True Self and decided to dedicate your life to kicking the shit out of people, but what's your background? What was your life before you became a professor?'

Big Vince took a sip from his non-alcoholic hip flask. He hadn't been sick for hours and his stomach was feeling neglected.

'Spent a guid bit o' ma childhood wi' ma Aunt Bertha. She stayed in a wee basement in a dairk cobbled close. It was a pairt o' the city where the street lamps were wiltin' an' even the graffiti had faded. Lang fingers and thick grey hair and sharp dentures, Aunt Bertha had, and she wore this plastic apron wi' a heraldic thingummy on it – witch an' cauldron rampant passant sable over field gules. Da said she shouldae been kept in an attic so's her cackling wid scare the woodworm away, but even Da had to admit the pies she made tae her secret recipe were like nae other. She wouldnae move intae nae attic, though. Happy in her basement, wiz Aunt Bertha, because her best friend lived next door. None ae us ever met him, mind. They said he used tae be a barber.'

Selina mused about the lasting effects of childhood influences, but before she could inquire further into Big Vince's early life, he'd turned aside and vomited.

'Och, that's better,' he said, wiping his lips. 'Ye cannae whack a guid boak.'

'Do you have Australian ancestry?' wondered Gabriella, startled into glancing round at her companions by the cry of "Ruth".

'Naw, I dinnae ken ony Ozzie relatives, but I dinnae see why a gang o' criminal-descended Colonials should hae a monopoly on boakin.'

'Not among *my* favourite pastimes,' said Selina, her lips prim again. 'It reminds me of my sojourn in hospital. The meals I received seemed to consist mainly of emetics.' Then she caught sight of Cuthbert's rusting yellow car, half-capsized in the ditch, and of the hat on its passenger seat. Sudden fury blossomed on her cheeks. 'My hat!' she cried. 'I knew it had been stolen! Wait 'til I get my hands on the owner of this car!'

Sniffer Simon's nose examined the wheels of the Volkswagen.

'Unless I'm mistaken, Ms Crumpett, which I'm not,' he said, 'the owner of this car is going to have the shit kicked out of him before your hands can be got on him.'

~

HOSPITAL FOOD

Those who're acquainted with hospital food,
As I fear has been my lot,
Might consider me not unduly rude
When experience forces me to conclude
That the menu comprises growths and glands
Extracted by expert surgeons' hands
From patients long forgot.

What we observe when the canteen door opens
Would make any passer-by spew;
You note, while attempting with care and caution
To savour the flavour of pickled abortion,
It passes the powers of the English language
To describe the taste of an abscess sandwich
Or the texture of tumour stew.

Indeed, you may say of our canteen men
That they suffer from lack of taste,
But despite a boiled spleen now and then,
And cream of specimen soup again,
And flavours and odours that pass us by,
And textures we'd hate to identify,
At least they're preventing waste.

~

Patricia and Herr Dr von Tür seek directions

Herr Dr von Tür entered the dry bar of *The Jolly Jihadi* and began to converse with al-Bert and al-Gernon, both of whom proved to be suffering from psychosexual imbalances involving fantasies about goats. Patricia was consigned to the women's quarters at the back of the hostelry. She had the foresight to cover her head, arms and legs before she entered.

In the semi-darkness, a woman in a burkha was shouting into her mobile phone.

'Why do you always pick the cheesecake? Why not a fresh fruit salad, which is healthier? Why not try a chocolate sponge, or rice pudding with apricots? You could order sticky toffee pudding if you wanted, not that I'd touch it because it's disgusting, or you could pretend to be a bit more up-market for once and ask for the crème brulée, but no, it's always the cheesecake – raspberry cheesecake, Bailey's cheesecake, white chocolate cheesecake, gorgonzola cheesecake, pepperoni cheesecake, whatever's on the menu, it's got to be cheesecake, always the cheesecake. You're so *boring*, so *predictable*. Why do I bother? Cheesecake, cheesecake! Has your capacity to consider alternative desserts deserted you? Has any such capacity, if you ever had it, withered in the mental desert between your ears? If you go on and on choosing cheesecake every time you dine out, you'll get your just deserts one of these days … What do you *mean*, you're giving up on desserts?'

The woman gave an exasperated squeak and slammed down the phone. She'd have hidden her face in her hands if it hadn't been hidden already.

'Nightmare, aren't they?' said Patricia, sitting beside her.

'Tell me about it. He's a total arsehole. All four of us are fed up with his eating habits. His goats are pissed off with him, too.'

'How do you know the goats' opinions?'

'They never stop bleating about him. And as for the camels …' The woman in the burkha studied Patricia. 'Ah. An infidel. I suppose you're surprised to hear one of a man's four wives haranguing him over the phone in such–'

Goats *and* camels? *And* four wives? Wealthy enough, thought Patricia. He could afford much more up-market deserts than cheesecake, or even crème brulée.

'Some frustrations are transcultural. Sorry to have intruded on your private rant, but I've come to ask for help. I need to find a woman called Selina Crumpett, a one-time marathon runner and an authority on gnomes. I believe she lives in Rotting Bishop or somewhere near. Do you know her?'

The woman shook the top of her burkha.

'No. The name means nothing to me. I suppose she's another infidel.'

'I don't know her religious affiliation, if any. Do you think someone else here …?'

The burkha shrugged again.

'Need to ask one of the men. *They* can go out and tour the village and its surroundings; *we* can't, except on leash.'

Patricia wondered how she could contrive to contact one

of the men in order to ask him where she might find Selina Crumpett, since being of the female persuasion she was confined to a man-free room. However, her phone rang before the woman in the burkha could answer.

'I have the directions ascertained,' said Herr Dr von Tür, 'so if to the outside of this building we now return, we can our departure make.' There was a pause, in which Patricia heard a smile. 'Also, I have six new patients with psychosexual imbalances acquired, and a terrorist plot that will exploding goats involve I have uncovered.'

'Oh, good,' said Patricia.

~

JIHADI SONG

We're awash with grand illusions,
We fill youngsters with delusions –
Make each youth and maiden barter
Future life for death as a martyr,
Volunteering with aplomb
To become a human bomb,
Spreading our younger generation
In soggy lumps across your nation.

If you fear us you're just mugs;
In the end we're merely thugs.
But beyond our terroristics,
We have other characteristics.
Though we gamble, we're not boozy,
And while Jihadis with an Uzi –
Contrary to common rumour –
Are devoid of sense of humour,
They just can't forbear to smile
When from them you run a mile.

A meeting to disturb the peace

Beside the front door of the long single-storey thatched cottage overlooking the strand, Cuthbert sat on the stone mushroom, absorbing the warmth of the sun, the scent of the flowers and the humming of bees. While Cuthbert counted butterflies, Gardner-Carpenter was hoeing flower beds, sweeping leaves and singing his song, the one with the dismal melody and indecipherable words. The susurrus of waves on the foreshore remained somnolent and the ferns and lichens adorning thatch and wall glowed in the afternoon sunlight, but a subtle dissonance had perturbed the idyll. The cat wasn't visible but its presence remained tangible. The sulphurous aroma from the well had intensified. And Yggdrasilsdottir's higher branches waved to the rhythm of Gardner-Carpenter's song, without benefit of breeze.

Cuthbert was throwing the door key from hand to hand, recalling his dream of the falling star and trying to ignore the dissonant note in the atmosphere, when he heard voices: walkers on the coastal path. He pocketed the key and stared at the gate. Gardner-Carpenter continued to hoe and sing.

'This is the place,' said Gabriella.

'Where the hat thief lives?' said Selina.

'Where I'll find the wee rat whit's needin' the shit kicked oot o' him?' said Big Vince.

'Indeed,' said Sniffer Simon, 'this is where you'll find the aforesaid debtor.'

'The place where at last I shall find my True Self,' said

Gabriella. She opened the gate, stepped on to the garden path, saw Gardner-Carpenter and froze. '*You! Scurvy knave, vile scoundrel, vermin, handbag thief! I swore I'd see you in Hell ere you fled Sniggerswick!*'

Gardner-Carpenter dropped his hoe and ran for cover but he was nowhere near quick enough. Consigning her leather case to the care of Big Vince, and unimpeded by her feminine clothes, Gabriella pursued her enemy, caught him beside a late-flowering azalea and started to kick the shit out of him. Big Vince was impressed.

'Yeeoowwww!' said Gardner-Carpenter. 'Aaarrrgghh!'

'Ruritanian,' thought Cuthbert, 'is an expressive tongue. Or perhaps we're hearing a simulacrum of the precursor of language that pre-dated poetry.'

'That girl has hidden depths,' said Selina.

'Aye. Merchant & Grendel could use her. But I cannae see nae Cuthbert Fell, Sniffer Simon.'

'I can't see anyone except Gabriella and the man out of whom she's kicking the shit,' said Selina, staring at the stone mushroom with Cuthbert sitting on it. 'I suppose your target must be inside the cottage, Vince, but I'm surprised he hasn't come out to investigate the commotion.'

'I fear you're mistaken, Ms Crumpett' said Sniffer Simon. 'Big Vince's quarry is right here.'

He trotted to the stone mushroom and urinated on it. Cuthbert dodged the stream and voiced his disgust, whereupon Selina and Big Vince noticed him. Big Vince said, 'Aha,' put on his de luxe knuckledusters and stepped forward; but contrary to Sniffer Simon's prediction, Selina was quicker.

'*You scurvy knave, you vile scoundrel, you vermin, you hat thief!* How dare you drive around with my hat on your car's passenger seat without returning it to me? And how did you come to steal it anyway?'

She started to kick the shit out of Cuthbert, who responded by expressing himself in Ruritanian. Selina seemed to have rediscovered her athletic prowess, though kick-boxing had never been among her specialisms.

'Aye, an angry woman can save a man a lot ae effort,' said Big Vince, sitting on the lawn beside the leather case and grinning metallically. 'Selina's daein' as guid a job as I'd dae myself, forbye she's kickin' different bits.'

But Gabriella interrupted Selina's exertions and *a fortiori* Big Vince's entertainment. Having reduced Gardner-Carpenter to a moaning foetal-position wreck beside the azalea, she'd deduced that since Selina was kicking the shit out of someone, that someone must be present.

'Selina, stop a minute. Please.' She looked at the body lying in the pool of mangy dog urine beside the stone mushroom. 'Are you Cuthbert Fell?'

Cuthbert moaned.

'Two moans for yes,' said Gabriella, 'one moan for no. Are you Cuthbert Fell?'

'Moan moan.'

'Right. Where's the pyramid?'

Selina and Big Vince stared at each other.

'Pyramid? What pyramid?' they chorused in different accents.

'Moan!' said Gardner-Carpenter, and burst into tears.

~

Abdul returns, with company

Spiritually uplifted by the Hajj, his mind full of the good deeds to which he intended to devote the rest of his life, Abdul decided he needed a holiday. Indonesia was a predominantly Muslim country and he was halfway there already, so it seemed the ideal destination. Once in Indonesia he sought out Bali. On a beach in Bali he met Aniles and, having discovered that she pronounced her name "An-ill-ease", with the stress on the middle syllable, he fell in love with her. They climbed Mount Agong together and admired the long-tailed monkeys. They held hands and immediately beheld a firework display, or possibly a volcanic eruption.

'I wish to marry you,' said Abdul.

'I'm not a Muslim,' said Aniles. 'I'm a Christian, though not a very devout one. So would you be allowed to marry me?'

'Yep. Praise be to Allah, there's a ruling to that effect in the Holy Quran, specifically in al-Maa'idah 5:4. Imam al-Tabari interpreted the verse as meaning that I'm permitted to marry a free woman who's either Jewish and believes in the Torah, or Christian and believes in the Gospel; provided she's chaste. And as far as I know no one's challenged Imam al-Tabari's interpretation. So I'm allowed. Provided ...'

Abdul bit his lip. Aniles squeezed his hand and evinced happiness. Then she squeezed his hand again and evinced doubt and concern. Abdul realised that when a man wishes to live with a woman, he has to come to terms with a lot of contradictory evincing. He asked what was wrong.

'I might not be who or what you think I am, Abdul.'

They stood on the highest peak in Bali and looked out over land and sea. Allah in His goodness has created such a beautiful world for His servants, thought Abdul, and Bali and Aniles are the most beautiful parts of it. In His infinite mercy He's made earthquake zones and active volcanoes, too, not to mention West Nile virus and childhood leukaemia.

'You're yourself,' he said. 'Nothing else matters to me.'

'A sweet thing to say but not true. I'm not just myself. I'm also another woman's True Self.'

This left Abdul at a loss for words, proving beyond doubt that he was a man conversing with a woman. After a minute he stuttered: 'Then whose True Self are you, and where can we find her?'

Aniles told him. The woman whose True Self she was shared her name, she explained, except it was spelt backwards.

'Then we must go backwards to England and find her so you can become your own real self. I need to return there anyway because I must discover what's become of my friend Cuthbert, who will surely need rescuing by this time.'

'Rescuing? From what?' said Aniles.

'From himself, mostly. Cuthbert's talented but he's a walking disaster area. Or, more commonly, a falling-over disaster area. Most people dismiss him as insignificant, which he isn't. He can be a total dick, though.'

So Abdul and Aniles returned hand in hand to Britain. They found Cuthbert's bedsit under new occupancy and there was no forwarding address, though one of the neighbours mentioned Big Vince's visit and showed Abdul the Merchant & Grendel business card. Abdul's heart sank. He phoned Merchant & Grendel but learned only that Big Vince had gone to find the elusive Mr Fell and had not yet returned.

'If you find Mr Fell, we'll be most grateful if you'll tell us his whereabouts,' said the director, Mr Merchant. 'Or alternatively, if you find Big Vince, tell *him*.'

Abdul offered no assurance.

'Well, I can't find Cuthbert, my beloved, but we can still go to find Selina,' he told Aniles. 'Since you're her True Self, it will be interesting to see what ensues.'

'Yes,' said Aniles. She smiled, though the prospect frightened as well as excited her.

They made their way to Rotting Bishop and sought directions.

'Why not ask in there?' said Aniles, pointing to *The Jolly Jihadi*. 'To judge from the name it's run by Muslims, who will surely help you.'

'The name suggests it's run by jerks and knob-heads,' said Abdul, 'and I don't want to ask jerks and knob-heads for help.'

As they spoke, two people emerged from *The Jolly Jihadi*: a large woman in her late middle years wearing a dress that resembled a parachute on hallucinogens, and a man of similar age wearing pince-nez and a suit as old as him. The man made a pronouncement with a verb at the end; it had something to do with exploding goats. The woman replied, 'Oh, good. So now we know where to find Selina.'

Hearing the exchange, Aniles stepped forward.

'Excuse me. Did you say Selina? Selina Crumpett, perchance? We're looking for her. If you know–'

'Why, what a *coincidence*! You're looking for Selina, too? How splendid! Perhaps we can travel together. I'm Patricia; I'm a priest. This is Herr Dr von Tür; he's a psychotherapist. I take it you're a friend of Selina's?'

'I'm her True Self. My name is Aniles. This is Abdul. We met in Bali and fell in love. Abdul is looking for a friend who's disappeared.'

'Many consultations are I think therefore needed,' said Herr Dr von Tür. 'We shall begin to consult as we four together towards Forlorn House journey.'

Abdul frowned.

'Herr Dr von Tür? My friend who's disappeared is Cuthbert Fell. I believe he's consulted you several times. Do you know where–?'

'Aha! It is another twist in the ribbon! The Celtic knot still greater intricacy attains!'

～

COINCIDENCE

Coincidence? It might be so,
Coincidences come and go.
You say, 'Coincidence? I think not!
Life is indeed a Celtic knot!
Fortuitous association
Indicates predestination –
Though the evidence won't convince
Tolstoyan sceptics like Big Vince.
Remember, when you got that bill
For fifty pounds, which made you ill,
You got a gift that selfsame day
Of just the sum you had to pay?'
Oh, sure. Compelling evidence.
No such thing as coincidence.
It takes a Higher Power to place
Two holes in every feline face
Just where the cat's eyes are located;
Marvel and be fascinated!
It must make you feel quite chipper
When you note that Jack the Ripper
And Attila the Hun, it's true,
And others share with Winnie the Pooh
The selfsame middle name! By gosh!
Coincidence? What utter bosh!

The Cat of Doom reappears

'You're an electronic engineer, so take it apart and tell me how it works.'

Gabriella pointed at the pyramid, which, although not plugged in, glowered back at her. Cuthbert glanced from one to another and crept forward. Selina, Big Vince and Sniffer Simon formed a rapt audience beside the door, and the three became four when Gardner-Carpenter crawled his bruised way to the threshold.

Gabriella studied the rest of the room. On the wall hung a photograph of a man she recognised as Edmund Dawson Rogers, nineteenth century spiritualist, mesmerist and co-founder of the Society for Psychical Research, complete with tweed jacket, moustache and a shooting stick; probably taken in Switzerland, where he liked to ramble. There was also a photograph of Mount Ararat, where Noah's Ark had come to rest. On the chest of drawers sat a trio of early twentieth century teddy bears: Richard Steiff's 55 PB design, she noted, assumed lost in a shipwreck and therefore priceless. The ticket to the Eastbourne performance of *Brigadoon* was perhaps a clue to something, though it wasn't clear what.

Gabriella looked inside the wardrobe. The item of bed-linen was of little interest.

'Hello, Bruce,' she said.

The seven-legged spider nodded a greeting.

Cuthbert made a puzzled noise. He had detached one face of the pyramid, with (strange to relate) no obvious injury to either the artefact or himself, and was staring in disbelief at the internum.

'It's empty,' he said. 'There are no electronic components at all. The mains lead enters through the side, here, but it just – well, ends. In mid air. Yet when you plug the pyramid in …'

'So you still don't know how it works,' said Gabriella.

'It *can't* work. There's nothing to *make* it work. Nothing to do anything!'

'Och, it's jist a wee bit o' carpentry whit somebody's pit a lead intae fir a laugh,' said Big Vince.

'Not carpentry,' wheezed Gardner-Carpenter. 'Cabinet making.'

'Pedantic wee git, are ye no'? Right, Mr Fell, enough o' yer tinkerin' wi' yon toy. Come oan oot here so I can kick the shit oot o' ye, if Selina's left ony in ye tae kick.'

Cuthbert replaced the triangular panel so the pyramid's non-existent mechanism was hidden from view.

'The present matter is more important than any attempt at debt collection, Professor,' said Gabriella.

'Aye, mebbe it is fir you, Ms de Clare, but I've ma job tae dae.'

Big Vince adjusted his knuckleduster and stepped forward. Cuthbert plugged in the pyramid and dived for cover under the bed. The red light glowed. Big Vince stopped in his tracks.

'If there's naethin' inside yer box, why's yon light shinin', ye lyin' wee git?'

'Odd smell,' said Selina.

Sniffer Simon yelped, spun round and fled from the garden. Terror fuelled his legs. Never in his life had he galloped so fast.

'Where's he away tae in sich a hurry?' wondered Big Vince.

'Grzgrtskya!' Gardner-Carpenter's voice had returned to full volume despite his battered rib cage. 'Dar flkn fyelliski revidit!'

He pointed at the bathroom door. The cat was framed against it, motionless, eyes yellow and malevolent. Everyone took a step backwards, except Gabriella, who opened her leather case. The others wondered how, since the case was unopenable. She reached inside and drew out something shiny.

Selina pointed at the pyramid.

'Look! It's getting bigger! It's growing!'

She was right. The pyramid was getting bigger. And bigger. So was the cat.

~

Herr Dr von Tür is once again bewildered

Most road users perceive an elderly driver wearing a hat as a slow-moving menace, not least if the car is a Mercedes, and particularly if the hat resembles a demoralised pancake embellished with an artificial pink rose and lacy bits. So perhaps it was no coincidence that Patricia drove with exaggerated care and ignored the lengthening tail of impatience behind her.

'Bloody hell,' muttered Abdul, cowering in the back seat beside Aniles, expecting at any moment to be blown to pieces by volleys of frustration puncturing the rear window.

Herr Dr von Tür twitched in the passenger seat and wondered what buried memories had elicited the twitch. The thought distracted him from his confusion about True Selves. Once, he wasn't sure how long ago, someone had asked him, 'Don't you want to find *your* True Self?' and the question had flung him into a fugue state. He was still trying to come to terms with it. An unrelated twitch was the ideal way to distract himself.

'Patience, everyone,' said Aniles. 'It's not as though a crisis is imminent.'

By the time they reached Mangy Dog Farm and heard the familiar disharmonious unison – *We're mangy dogs in a close-knit pack/ And we take and eat whatever we lack* – the queue of traffic behind them had thinned to almost nothing as driver after driver opted for alternative and less lugubrious routes.

'This is surely the farm of mangy dogs, so if correct guidance we have received, close to Forlorn House we now must be,' said Herr Dr von Tür.

The psychotherapist's companions offered no comment. Patricia drove on, the Mercedes murmuring refined objections to its *adagio doloroso* pace and politely deprecating the roughness of the track.

'There,' said Abdul. 'Just ahead, on the left. The white poplar and the rowan.'

'Well spotted,' said Patricia. *A rowan*, she thought. *Ah, how significant rowans were to me in my days as Regnarta!* She piloted the car on to the drive of Forlorn House and braked to a gentle halt. Everyone alighted and walked towards the front door.

'Sorry to disappoint you, folks,' said a deep voice, 'but you've come at a bad time. There's nobody at home except me and these trees, and as you can see we're in the garden not the house, which is locked.'

The four visitors looked around. They saw no one. Then the invisible light bulb began to glow above the head of Aniles.

'Ah! Hello! Er – we came to see Selina. Do you know where …?'

'Yes. She isn't far away.' Smiley studied Aniles without moving his eyes, his pipe, or any other portion of his plastic self. 'You're her True Self, aren't you? A-ha. Well, I suppose most women's True Selves are much younger than their real selves. Pleased to meet you, anyway. I'm Smiley.'

Aniles introduced herself and her fellow-travellers. Patricia stepped forward with the file she'd lifted from the Assistant Manager's grey filing cabinet.

'Hello, Smiley. I'm Patricia. Do you recognise these documents?'

'Of course I do. They comprise a detailed account of a stitch-up that is likely soon to prove the undoing of the humans who perpetrated it, and of a lot more humans and other creatures besides. Might be too late to do anything about it now. But it's interesting that you've discovered the file, Patricia, intact and complete. According to reports, it had been lost beyond hope of recovery. How convenient.'

Herr Dr von Tür stared at the sky and his twitch returned. True Selves? A talking plastic garden ornament? A lethal stitch-up involving a long lost file? None of this was possible. He knew he was sane, so plainly the rest of the world was mad: a straightforward logical inference. It was as he'd always suspected.

'Why do you say it might be too late?' Abdul frowned.

'Where's Selina gone?' asked Aniles.

'Are you all right, Doctor?' Patricia was solicitous.

Before any of those questions could be answered, Esmerelda and Winston began to wave their branches as though a high wind had sprung up among them. They'd received an urgent message from Yggdrasilsdottir. Smiley understood it.

'Oh, bloody hell, here we go,' he said. 'Right: Selina has gone to the thatched cottage along the track. Ms Gabriella de Clare and Professor Vincent Tacitus McGrotty went with her. According to the tree telegraph, which functions at a higher level than the bush telegraph, a person styled Gardner-Carpenter was already in residence there, along with a Mr Cuthbert Fell.'

'Cuthbert!' shouted Abdul. 'Let's go, quickly, before this implausible sequence of coincidences evolves into disaster!'

From Mangy Dog Farm, the howl of Jerry Mire was borne on the air to their wondering ears: 'Wooooooooooooooooooo ooeeeeeeeeeeeeeeeeeee! Wooooooooooeeeeeeeeeeeeee! The Cat of Doom hath been let out of the bag again! Lo, this is a proper bummer!'

'See what I mean?' said Abdul. 'Whatever this Cat of Doom is, it doesn't sound like good news.'

'It isn't, Abdul,' said Smiley. 'Your friend Cuthbert Fell has let it out of the bag. The evolution of the series of implausible coincidences into disaster is about to reach its culmination. One might almost say "conclusion".'

Revelations

A sustained growl emanated from Yggdrasilsdottir's high branches. An answering growl emanated from the expanding cat. Gabriella turned her back on the company, deserted her leather case and strode towards the pyramid, shiny object in hand. By this time, the apex of the pyramid had pierced the thatched roof. The fumes from the well in the garden had grown visibly noxious.

'Och, I'm needin tae boak again,' said Big Vince, sniffing the air and swigging from his flask.

'No time for that,' said Selina. 'Come on, Vince, we need to fetch Smiley before things start to crawl, ooze, slither and scuttle from the depths of that well!'

The pyramid thrust its way skywards and the cottage roof disintegrated. Fragments of thatch and a host of insects rained down.

'Whit's a plastic gnome supposed tae dae aboot ony o' this shite?' said Big Vince.

'If we can persuade him in time, he'll summon the Gnome Guard! Come on, move!'

Selina's limbs went into half-remembered marathon mode. Big Vince lumbered in her wake, complaining between gasps about the thievin' wee rat whit hadnae had aw the shit kicked oot o' him yet. Cuthbert was relieved by his departure but the relief was overshadowed by his anxiety about the now gigantic Cat, the destruction of the cottage that had become his home, and the strange behaviour of Gabriella.

The pyramid had acquired a visible entrance. The entrance was still small but it was expanding, like the cat; and as Gabriella approached, either it grew to accommodate her or she shrank so she could be accommodated. A moment later she'd vanished into the pyramid's internum.

The Cat rose to its feet. It yawned, stretched, surveyed the tiny humans retreating from before its face, and adopted an imminent-pounce pose. It licked its lips with a tongue the size of a stair-carpet and its barbed wire whiskers twitched.

Then Gabriella re-emerged from the pyramid. Cuthbert watched, as though in a dream, remembering Gardner-Carpenter's claim that the entrance to a pyramid signifies the quest for one's True Self, the integration of Self and Soul, of Individual Consciousness with Universal Consciousness. Gabriella was now dressed from head to toe in white, a white brilliant enough to shame every magnesium flare and washing powder advert in the world, and there was a gold circlet on her head. The shiny thing in her hand had become a sword and it shone with merciless light.

'Found her True Self, I suppose,' said Cuthbert.

'Gabriella de Clare.' Gardner-Carpenter sounded reflective, offering a mental mirror to the situation. 'For "de Clare" read "pronounce", "proclaim"… or "trumpet"… Ah, trumpet! And for Gabriella, read Gabriel!'

The Cat sprang from the remains of the cottage, out of the garden, away from the vision in blinding white and its merciless blade, and splashed into the sea. Then it turned to face the shore, prepared for battle. Apart from its yellow eyes and white fangs it was as black as interstellar space. Those who looked upon it imagined they saw a huge cat-shaped hole in the sky through which the darkness of infinity poured.

'I thought the Archangel Gabriel was male,' said Cuthbert.

'Gender neutral,' said Gardner-Carpenter. 'Read Pseudo-Dionysius the Areopagite or Thomas Aquinas: three spheres or hierarchies of angels, each comprising three orders or choirs, all of them gender-neutral. Or if you prefer, sexless.'

Gabriel(la) strode sword in hand to the shore to confront the Cat. The phrase 'Not a cat in Hell's chance' flitted through Cuthbert's mind.

'Seraphim, Cherubim, Thrones or Elders,' continued Gardner-Carpenter; 'then Dominions or Lordships, Virtues or Strongholds, Powers or Authorities ...'

Gabriel(la) raised her/his sword. The Cat flicked its tail, sending tidal waves crashing into the Sussex coast, blasting lumps of chalk replete with Late Cretaceous fossils out of the cliffs.

'... and finally, Principalities or Rulers, Archangels, Angels,' said Gardner-Carpenter. 'Of course, Clement of Rome, St Ambrose, St Jerome, Gregory the Great and other luminaries of the early Church proposed variants of this list of–'

'Gardner-Carpenter,' said Cuthbert, 'shut up.'

The Cat rose to its full height, dwarfing Gabriel(la), who looked tiny and helpless before it but at the same time white and indomitable. The Cat lifted its right forepaw, all its six-foot-long claws unsheathed. Gabriel(la) thrust her sword at it and drew black blood. The Cat leapt backwards, sending a minor tsunami in the direction of France. Its ears flattened and its mouth opened in a sky-rending scream.

'Quite a battle,' said Gardner-Carpenter. 'It has an air of Finality.'

'Ah'm a-geddin' sick an' tired of your asides,' said Cuthbert in an unconvincing Transatlantic drawl.

The fumes from the well grew thicker. Noises became audible from below: crawling, oozing, slithering, scuttling noises. Cuthbert and Gardner-Carpenter retreated. The battle between Gabriel(la) and the Cat of Doom raged on.

A blackbird sang a disgruntled accompaniment to the conflict.

~

HAPPY APOCALYPSE, WORLD!

Has the Earth just tilted or has our balance altered,
Is the ground a-tremble or have our knee joints faltered?
Our species has wrought havoc now
for far too many days
And so the world seeks vengeance
for the errors of our ways.

The Cat of Armageddon's bringing horrors in its wake,
The well will vomit demons as the earth begins to quake.
We'll try to hide ourselves away, but nowhere safe is found
As our histories fall about our ears on ever-shifting ground.

The smell of sulphur fills the air, boiling from pits of Hell,
It's really most unpleasant and it makes us feel unwell,
Apocalyptic creatures rise in fire to torture everyone
And merry little devils come to join in all the fun.

What can a few lost humans do when th' world
has had its chips
But stick their fingers in the dyke of the Apocalypse?
Our species needs assistance this catastrophe to quell
But whence will this assistance come?
Ah, time and tide may tell.

~

Ancient battles recalled

Big Vince tried to sprint but only managed to become breathless. He couldn't keep pace with Selina, who seemed to run without effort, as she'd done years before. Before she reached her home, with Big Vince lumbering in her wake, she met the quartet of visitors heading in the opposite direction.

'Selina!' Patricia's arms threatened a suffocating embrace and her smile was a crescent moon. 'You won't remember me. I'm Patricia now, but I was once Renarta, and I entered your childhood bedroom as a flying–'

'Rabbit,' said Selina. 'Yes, I remember. Very nice, but there are more pressing–'

'I know, I know, that's all in the past. *This* is what matters now – look! I've found the report of the gnomes' grievances, the report on the investigation you initiated after the Remembrance Day revolt, the report everyone said was–'

'Lost,' said Selina. 'Right. Good. Well done Renarta. Patricia. Smiley needs to see it. And I need to see Smiley because we have an apocalypse to avert.' She caught sight of Patricia's companions. 'Who–?'

Selina's lack of interest in how and where the report had been found deflated Patricia, but only for a moment. She introduced Herr Dr von Tür, who bowed formally and pondered the sort of psychosexual imbalance that could a woman to run a mini-marathon cause. Then she presented Abdul and Aniles.

'Aniles?' The surprise deflected Selina from her purpose for almost ten seconds. 'Aniles, my True Self? All the way from Bali? What brings you here?'

Aniles began to explain her fiancé Abdul's urge to find his friend Cuthbert before disaster befell him, but the ground began to shake beneath her and spray from giant tidal waves fell around them.

'Quickly, True Self!' Selina's urgency was redoubled. 'Back to Forlorn House! We must see Smiley and persuade–'

'But we have so much to talk about!' cried Aniles.

'I think this Cat of Doom has to take priority, darling,' said Abdul. 'Cuthbert's in trouble.'

Herr Dr von Tür nodded. The young man was right; it was obligatory that he act. Cuthbert Fell was his patient. If in trouble his patient was, beside the patient he must be. On the thought, he started to walk in the direction of the once-idyllic cottage, now the location of a pyramid. The pyramid was a hundred and fifty feet high and growing.

Herr Dr von Tür's departure was ignored by all.

'Did ye say "Cat o' Doom"?' gasped Big Vince, avoiding collision with the psychotherapist and lumbering up to Abdul.

'Yes. Smiley the gnome said it was seriously bad news.'

'Aye. Seen it. Muckle great mingin' moggy if ever there wiz. Need tae dae somethin' aboot it.'

'Like what?' Abdul glanced around as another tremor shook the earth, branches fell from trees and more sea spray descended. 'Look, under these circumstances, I can't leave my fiancée to–'

'Look, laddie, she's jist found the woman whose True Self

she is. They've a lot tae talk aboot. An' Selina said somethin' aboot rousin' the Gnome Guard. Best leave 'em tae it, son, an' get this Cat o' Doom sorted.'

Abdul shook his head.

'Hold on. Don't I know you?' Big Vince, he observed, was carrying a copy of the latest *History Today*. 'Aren't you me in reverse?'

'Dinnae ken whit ye mean. Thing is, we need tae–'

'Listen: as a kid, I used to go around kicking the shit out of everybody. Now I've found religion and I'm studying history. You used to go to the Kirk every Sunday, didn't you? And unless I'm mistaken you taught history, and then you gave it all up for a job–'

'Kickin' the shit oot of folk whit needs it,' said Big Vince. 'Aye, right, so one ae us is the ither yin's True Self, or upside doon self, or somethin' o' the kind. Big deal. Let's dae whit needs daein': deal wi' this Cat o' Doom.'

Abdul shook his head. He was beginning to feel as though the ground beneath his feet had become insecure, which as a matter of fact it had. It shook again to prove the point.

'How?'

'Think, laddie. Whit hates cats? Most ancient o' mammalian battles?'

'Dogs, I suppose.'

'Right. An' where roond here can we find a pack o' dogs whit jist happen tae be pals o' mine?'

From the garden of Forlorn House, a rowan, a white poplar, two women and a gnome noted that Abdul and Big Vince were running away in the direction of Rotting Bishop.

'Where're they going?' chorused Selina and Aniles.

'Going to the dogs, the pair of them,' said Smiley. 'But as for your proposal, or request, or whatever it was …'

'Special pleading,' said Aniles and Selina.

'Okay. Well, the answer is: why should I? Or rather, why should *we*?'

'Because it's your role, the role of the gnomes,' said the women.

'Whether Greek,' said Aniles,

'Or Norse,' said Selina.

'And what about recompense? Recognition? A nice "thank you", for example?' said Smiley.

'We have the report again now, Smiley,' said Selina.

'We can lobby parliament and insist that all the recommendations be implemented,' said Aniles.

'We can get Hollywood to make a disaster film illustrating what happens if gnomes are ignored,' said Selina.

'We can even allow them to call the film a "movie",' said Aniles.

Smiley pondered. The ground shook with renewed vigour. Tiles fell from the roof of Forlorn House and there was the sound of cups and medals falling out of display cabinets.

'Lend me your phone again, Selina,' he said. 'I'll call our gnominated leaders. No promises, mind.'

~

Ancient battles rejoined

Herr Dr von Tür paused. Should he, he wondered, to the institution for the bewildered return? The idyllic cottage he had entered earlier lay now in ruins. The pyramid erecting itself from the cottage's remains had swollen beyond the dreams of Freud. Just offshore, a giant Cat was locked in battle with a sword-bearing archangel. Recurrent tremors afflicted the earth. There was a heavy sulphurous stench and a menacing cacophony of crawling, oozing, slithering, scuttling. What, the psychotherapist demanded of himself, was causing him these Biblical manifestations to imagine? He had supposed that his personal psychosexual imbalances had back into balance been brought. Could he have mistaken been?

He squared his shoulders. It was necessary, he decided, all these impressive illusions to ignore. Somewhere in this scene of devastation was his patient, Cuthbert Fell, all-round failure and portaphobe; the man who had of letting the Cat of Doom out of the bag been accused, the man out of whom a Glaswegian with tattoos and piercings had vowed the shit to kick. It was imperative that he find him.

'Good afternoon,' said Gardner-Carpenter.

Herr Dr von Tür hoped the afternoon was good but he was yet to be convinced. A shower of sea spray soaked him, making him even more dubious. He polished his pince-nez and scrutinised Gardner-Carpenter.

'It is important that to Cuthbert Fell as soon as possible I speak. It seems he is with feelings of guilt afflicted.'

'So he should be,' said Gardner-Carpenter, as the earth shook again and the Cat of Doom yowled. 'Look what a mess he's made of the cottage by playing around with that pyramid. Letting *that* thing out.'

He pointed at the Cat, still held at bay in the bay by Gabriel(la).

'Ah,' said Herr Dr von Tür. 'It seems my apocalyptic illusions you share. A consultation with me you should request.'

The stench from the well became overpowering. Something slithered, or oozed, over its lip. Something else crawled.

'This might not be a good time,' said Gardner-Carpenter. 'The best thing we can do with this place is to get out of it with the utmost celerity. But we should try to lead Mr Fell away from the well first.'

Cuthbert was wandering around the wrecked garden with no evident sense of direction. Herr Dr von Tür deemed him in need of guidance.

'Did the latest thing that from the well emerged a slithering or a scuttling make?' he wondered.

'I think it squelched,' said Gardner-Carpenter, 'when Mr Fell trod on it. Mr Fell! Your psychotherapist has arrived!'

Cuthbert stumbled towards Herr Dr von Tür and Gardner-Carpenter, each of whom took him by an arm and started to lead him from the neighbourhood of the ruined cottage. But before they'd gone a hundred yards, a commotion approached from the direction of Rotting Bishop: scores of galloping paws and a disharmonious unison of canine voices chanting *We're mangy*

dogs in a close-knit pack/ And we take and eat whatever we lack/
We ain't got charm so if you chance your arm/ By causing harm …

As the three escapees turned to watch, the entire pack, led
by Mangy Dog One, charged into the sea, some to Gabriel(la)'s
left and some to her/his right, and beset the hind legs of the Cat
of Doom with bites, snarls, growls, nippings and worryings. At
the same time, Gabriel(la) thrust forward with her/his sword.

The Cat of Doom leapt into the air, snarling, all its fur
standing on end and its tail resembling what a bottle brush
might look like to someone who'd taken a heavy dose of LSD.
It fled inland and rushed up the trunk of Yggdrasilsdottir.
Yggdrasilsdottir swayed seawards, then thrashed her branches
landwards and flung the Cat head over paws through the air.
It soared along a parabolic trajectory with a yowl like a fleet
of fighter aircraft, shrinking as it flew. It sailed straight into the
well and disappeared.

Gardner-Carpenter applauded and started recite a well-
known Sniggerswick chant:

> *Ding, dong, bell,*
> *Pussy's gone to Hell.*
> *What put it in?*
> *Lots and lots of sin.*
> *What'll get it out?*
> *Nowt.*

He repeated the ditty and his companions joined in, the
blackbird supplying a descant that seemed a little less
disgruntled. The mangy dogs joined in, too, wagging their way

out of the sea and shaking droplets of water across the foreshore, lamenting the absence of passers-by to soak.

'Things are still coming out of the well,' said Cuthbert, 'so perhaps we ought to leave. But not without Gabriella! We have to save Gabriella!'

'I think Gabriella or Gabriel is more than capable of saving her or himself,' said Gardner-Carpenter. 'And as for the things coming out of the well, I suspect they're about to be put in their place.'

Even as he spoke, the Gnome Guard marched on to the scene armed with fishing rods, garden forks, coloured plastic boots and pointy hats. With Smiley Crumpett in their van they charged at the crawling, oozing, slithering, scuttling entities that were spreading outwards in concentric circles from their point of egress and drove them back into the nether depths, with a cacophony of squelching and puncturing. Within a quarter of an hour there was nothing left above ground to ooze, slither, scuttle or crawl, and the sulphurous aroma from below had diminished. The earth tremors dwindled and ceased.

The pyramid started to shrink. An hour later it had returned to its original size. By then, Gabriel(la) had returned to land and wrung most of the seawater out of her/his white outfit. She/he nodded to Cuthbert, glowered at Gardner-Carpenter and raised an inquiring eyebrow at Herr Dr von Tür.

'Where's my leather case? I can put this thing away now.' She/he waved the sword, removed the gold circlet from her/his head, wiped her/his brow and exhaled.

'And I could use a drink,' she/he added.

~

More tree talk

'Here's a strange affair, Esmerelda,' said Winston. 'Oaths of enduring friendship among mangy dogs, plastic gnomes and humans. Which of these species will be the first to break its promise?'

'Unlikely to be the dogs,' said Esmerelda, 'since I believe they're noted for fidelity as well as for urinating on trees.'

'Unlikely to be the gnomes,' said Winston, 'since their commitment to barring the gates of the chthonic has survived for centuries.'

The two trees fell silent. Salt water dripped from their leaves. The area around Forlorn House looked as though it had been hit by a falling star.

'Yggdrasilsdottir dealt with the Cat of Doom, didn't she?' said Esmerelda.

'Of course,' said Winston, 'but the human in white made a significant contribution, too, and the mangy dogs were quite brilliant.'

'Oh, I agree. But was the being in white merely human, or was it a human that had found its True Self?'

Winston surveyed the garden. The chestnut paling fence looked as though a score of bicycles had driven into it, and the lumps disfiguring the lawns and flower beds suggested the dedicated efforts of an army of large and energetic moles. The bird bath lay on its side. The humans were assembling around Smiley, who had returned to his accustomed place.

'I've often been struck by the resemblance between Selina and my cousin Lombardy,' said Winston.

'On the other hand, Selina's True Self has enough grace and delicacy of form to suggest a Birch.'

Winston nodded his upper twigs. Esmerelda was right, he thought: Aniles had the shape of a human that needed no coppicing or pollarding. In contrast, the two male humans in the gathering most nearly resembled an ageing Chile Pine and a sapling Cedar of Lebanon.

'Symmetry. I love symmetry,' he said, 'especially when Real Selves and True Selves are involved.'

Esmerelda sighed, displaying blossom.

'I believe I see what you mean. Selina has met Aniles, Real Self and True Self. Now all they have to do is to find out which is which. Aniles is preparing to couple with the young male with the darker bark, and the younger male is the complement of the older male whose bark is disfigured and tormented with paintings and nails and pins, and he in turn could be preparing to couple with Selina. Karma has graced the situation with symmetry. There was a similar manifestation of the grace of karma here not long ago. Perhaps it's something in the water.'

'But what about the larger female human that appears to be wrapped in a tent?' demanded Winston.

'Ah. Perhaps she's both Real Self and True Self, Renarta reconciled with Patricia. And I believe she's going to sing.'

Winston scanned the assembled humans again.

'I believe they are all going to sing,' he said. 'See, the older male with the disfigured bark, the one like a Chile Pine, has brought a musical device.'

Winston was right: Big Vince had brought the mandolin from his Aston Martin and was now tuning it. Patricia was distributing hymn sheets.

'At such a time as this,' she intoned, 'it is right for all of us to recall our youth, our innocence. Abdul, I hope you won't be offended by a small Christian celebration?'

Abdul glanced at the hymn sheet.

'Not at all,' he said. 'In any case, these words aren't specific to any religion. They'd be valid all over the world.'

CHILDREN'S HYMN

God made the little pine cone;
He made the tall pine tree;
He made the big strong lumberjack
to chop it down for me;

He made the pretty pulp mill,
the presses and the stains,
He made consumer markets
and all the retail chains,

and so the cardboard carton
to keep my cornflakes in,
and now He's made it all for me
I'll chuck it in the bin;

and so with all the works of God -
we'll pulp them up for trash:
our stomachs and our pockets lined
we'll dump them in the trash.

Herr Dr von Tür and the man with two pseudonyms

Gardner-Carpenter and Herr Dr von Tür stood where the gate had been, the gate from which wanderers along the coastal path had viewed the idyllic cottage and garden and wondered about the unseen occupant. Now the feline resident had gone, for good or ill. So had the cottage. Most of the garden, too.

Cuthbert was sitting on the stone mushroom, tossing from hand to hand a small shiny object that wasn't a sword, or even a fallen star, but the key to a door that no longer existed. He seemed content. Perhaps (suggested Gardner-Carpenter) recent events had caused Mr Fell's mind to withdraw from the world, to refuse to accept what his senses reported, but Herr Dr von Tür had a different explanation for his patient's new-found equanimity.

'The cause of his phobia has departed. He had from fear of doors all his life suffered, and now there is no door; the key alone remains. Therefore his psychosexual balance is restored.'

Gardner-Carpenter nodded.

'Ah. That helps to demystify him. On the other hand, what about her, or him?'

He pointed at Gabriel(la), who was foraging among the rubble. A seven-legged spider called Bruce scuttled past the two men, seeking new accommodation.

'The transformation we have witnessed is a most novel and effective way the psychosexual imbalance to resolve, since he or she that is sexless can no psychosexual imbalance have.' Herr Dr von Tür took off his pince-nez and began to chew them, indicating intense thought. 'The ideal partner for Cuthbert Fell is thus generated.'

Gardner-Carpenter explained that Gabriella had been far from sexless or gender-neutral when he'd stolen her handbag, or when she'd identified him and kicked the shit out of him by way of retribution. Herr Dr von Tür, intrigued by these references to things past, began to question his companion. As always, Gardner-Carpenter was happy to divulge details of his idiosyncratic history, in which Herr Dr von Tür found riches beyond the dreams of analysts: early life in Ruritania, a country that did not (and does not) exist; becoming a serial killer, obliged to emigrate when this hobby was noted by the authorities; after a brief flirtation with necrophilia, taking up handbag theft; and then leaving Sniggerswick, moving to Rotting Bishop and becoming a gardener and carpenter.

'And it was thus that your two pseudonyms you acquired?'

'I adopted the pseudonyms when I came to Britain,' said Gardner-Carpenter. 'In Sniggerswick I was called both 'Carpenter' and 'Gardener'. After I moved here, along with the blackbird and his family, I became the carpenter and the gardener, thus becoming a prime exemplar of either nominative or pseudonominative determinism. When Mr Fell heard about that part of my history he joined the two pseudonyms with a hyphen, thus welding together two formerly disparate parts of my personality. It enabled me to climb to a yet higher level of the pyramid.'

Herr Dr von Tür was disappointed to discover that his new

patient had resolved his own psychosexual imbalance without need for therapy, but he was no less intrigued by the history. Soon they were conversing about Gardner-Carpenter's favourite topics: the origin of language, the mysticism surrounding pyramids, and the character of gardens.

As they conversed, they ambled side by side in the direction of Rotting Bishop. By nightfall they had reached Forlorn House and joined the party comprising Selina, Aniles, Big Vince, Abdul and Patricia, bringing the total number of humans there assembled to seven. Both the new arrivals were able to reassure Abdul about Cuthbert's health and wellbeing, but they encouraged him to remain with his fiancée and stay away from the site of the thatched cottage.

'It seems likely that Mr Fell's life is acquiring a Significant Other,' explained Gardner-Carpenter, 'so he needs time alone with her or him'; and Herr Dr von Tür said the same, albeit with the main verb in a different place.

Smiley announced the imminence of storms, and Jerry Mire howled warnings from the back of Mangy Dog Farm, but the seven humans seemed too happy and content to listen; though Herr Dr von Tür began to recall one of his more disturbing dreams.

~

The four riders

'Ah! Here it is!'

Gabriel(la) lifted the leather case from a heap of old thatch and plaster. It was accompanied by the shattered portrait of a gentleman with moustache and shooting stick, three very dusty teddy bears and a broken wardrobe with no doors, yet it wasn't even scratched. More remarkably, the whiteness of Gabriel(la)'s robe was unsullied and undimmed. She/he opened the case and put the sword into it, withdrew another shiny metal object in its place and smiled at Cuthbert.

'Are you ready for this, Cuthbert Fell?'

'Ready for what?'

'For the final consequences of your bumbling incompetence. Of letting the Cat of Doom out of its pyramidal bag.'

'But *you* told me to open the pyramid!'

'I didn't tell you to switch it on.'

'I only switched it on to distract that Glaswegian thug from Merchant & Grendel!'

Gabriel(la) chuckled. Lightning split the sky around the horizon and thunder rolled.

'Did you indeed? Well, no matter. Happy Apocalypse!'

Gabriel(la) put the shiny object to her/his mouth. It was a silver trumpet. The blast she/he blew on it was quiet, yet it sounded for longer than Cuthbert could hold his breath and it seemed to fill the world.

'Quiet blast?' he thought. 'Oxymoron. Like "raging trickle" or "pantomime crankshaft".'

'Go to where the cottage gate used to be,' said Gabriel(la), 'and make ready to greet the new arrivals.'

Cuthbert went to the site of the gate. From amidst the ruins, Gabriel(la) watched as the four riders approached. She heard thunder rolling in the east, the west, the south and the north. A hot wind blew. Leaves fell. Crops withered.

'I wonder whether he'll understand what's happening,' she/he mused. 'What he plans to say to the riders is a matter for conjecture. I hope he won't greet them with quotations. But in the end it will make no difference even if he does.'

In the event, Cuthbert greeted the four riders succinctly.

'Hello,' he said.

'Good morning,' said the first rider, although it was late evening. The greeting sounded like a declaration of war.

'Good afternoon,' said the second. It reminded Cuthbert that he hadn't eaten all day and was hungry.

'Good evening,' said the third, and Cuthbert felt increasingly unwell.

'Good night,' said the fourth, and Cuthbert fell dead.

Gabriel(la) blew another blast on the silver trumpet, and events took their course.

~

In the end–

–there was total destruction. So in the beginning there will be nothing. Between those two – what? moments? events? (No, for reasons already stated) – between the end and the new beginning there was, is, and presumably will be, nothing becoming something.

It is therefore clear that a law of non-conservation of non-being must be added to the theoretical edifice of physics, and philosophy and religion will have to accommodate to it. *Ex nihil aliquid venit.* So much for the universe always being conservative.

Take Hawking radiation as the best-known manifestation of this new law of physics. A Bogoliubov transformation of a perfect vacuum generates a state in which there are pairs of particles and antiparticles. These annihilate each other instantaneously unless they're close to a black hole, in which case one of the pair is swallowed into the gravitational singularity and the other, relatively speaking, is emitted. To date, no one has observed this phenomenon, the thermal signature of which is miniscule in comparison to the black hole itself, but the theoretical prediction is indisputable.

Creativity is indeed rooted in destruction, so the physics of the vacuum in the vicinity of a black hole becomes a metaphor for human endeavour. The painter defaces a white canvas, the architect disfigures a green space, and the writer confronts a blank page and out of nowhere conjures a poem, a story, a doodle, a shopping list, a letter to someone half-forgotten. In all cases, blankness is suborned; the vacuum is awash with particles of energy. All is changed, all is in flux. There was something, then there was nothing, and change ceased; but in the future, near or remote, the seeds of creation latent in every episode of destruction will germinate.

Veni, creator spiritus. Discedite, mors.

~

Final fable

Four philosophers were discussing numbers.

'Why are so many human societies obsessed by the number seven?' said the first. 'Is it because there are seven days in a week or because there are seven deadly sins?'

There was a pause. Then the second philosopher said, 'Seven cardinal virtues, maybe.'

There was another pause. Then the third philosopher said, 'Something to do with Babylonian arithmetic. All of us are disciples of Babylon, like it or not.'

The fourth philosopher shook his head, setting up low-amplitude standing waves in his long white beard.

'Seven is the sum of Four and Three: the Number of Destruction and the Number of Creation. God created the world in six days and rested on the seventh, lest His works be condemned forever to comprise three days of production for every four of demolition. Consider the Pyramid.'

The other three philosophers were puzzled by this final remark. Why should they consider the Pyramid? The fourth philosopher stroked his long white beard, suppressing its undulations, and pontificated about four faces of the Pyramid and the triangular character of each face. The Pyramid is regarded as the home of Divine Fire, the source of creation and destruction, because it encapsulates and epitomises both. But the first three philosophers weren't impressed and deemed the fourth philosopher's exposition a load of horse shit.

They might have been more credulous had the total number of philosophers been three, not four; the Number of Creation, not the Number of Destruction.

But who knows?

About the Author

After he retired from a career in medicine and university teaching, Mark Henderson moved to the Peak District of Derbyshire, England, where he started to write fiction and to collect and tell local folktales.

Mark's previous two novels, National Cake Day in Ruritania and The Engklimastat, met with critical acclaim and the former was a contender for the Republic of Consciousness literary prize.

Mark has many publications to his name, long and short, covering many genres, including a collection of 62 traditional Peak District stories and a collection of performance pieces, Cruel and Unusual PunNishments.

Mark is secretary of his local creative writing group. He regularly performs at storytelling gigs and is in demand for his talks about his work and life experiences.

Find out more about Mark on his
website: www.markphenderson.com

If you have enjoyed this book, please consider leaving a review for Mark to let him know what you thought of his work.

You can find out more about Mark on his author page on the Fantastic Books Store. While you're there, why not browse our other delightful tales and wonderfully woven prose?

www.fantasticbooksstore.com